To all who care for the creatures

Keeper Of The Stars

Virginia Young

Riverhaven Books

www.RiverhavenBooks.com

Keeper of the Stars is a work of fiction. While some of the settings are actual, any similarity regarding names, characters, or incidents is entirely coincidental.

Published in the United States by Riverhaven Books, Massachusetts.

ISBN 978-1-951854-09-6

Designed by Stephanie Lynn Blackman
Whitman, MA

Chapter One

"Your last name is McGann?"

He smiled at the pretty blonde in the doorway then shrugged. "That's my name, Craig McGann."

Nell, one hand on her hip, the other at the door's edge, stood silent.

Craig stared at her questioning expression. "Is there a problem?"

Nell stared at her guest's intriguing features. Light brown hair, blue-grey eyes, a perfect jawline, and a slightly arrogant nose. She swallowed hard then shifted her weight from her right foot to both of her bare feet. "Do you know *my* name?"

Craig smiled. "No, but I will if you tell me."

"I'm Nell McGann."

"Small world," he offered. "Well, Ms. McGann, my grandfather is buried here, and I hoped to visit his grave."

"Your grandfather? No, it's impossible. I think you must be in the wrong place."

Craig looked lost.

Nell took pity on him and then shook her head. "What's his name? I know each one of these graves by heart. It's part of my duty as the owner of this cottage – I take care of the graves and the graves take care of me."

"Vincent William McGann. According to my father, my grandfather had an Army buddy with a family plot like this one. Before he died, he requested that instead of being buried at a national cemetery, he'd like his eternal rest to be near his good friend John."

"John Michael McGann was my grandfather. This answers the question I've had for a long while. I've planted daisies at the grave of Vincent McGann and never knew who he was. I'll need to look through my grandfather's folder again. He must have made note of this. He was meticulous with record keeping."

"From my understanding, my grandfather asked to be buried here since my grandmother wanted to be cremated, her ashes scattered in the Pacific. Your grandfather must have approved *my* grandfather's request."

"So you didn't attend the services."

Craig looked around at the beautiful meadows. "No, I was stationed in a war zone and couldn't make it back. Serving in the Army is kind of a family tradition. My father was here for the services. He flew in from the West Coast. It's been four years, but I'd like to pay my respects."

Nell took a deep breath. "Okay. Now that I think about it, I'm not surprised to hear that Grampa allowed

2

the burial of a friend. Many here are not McGanns, there's a mix of last names even though they're all related. I thought Vincent McGann was a distant relative, maybe a cousin. I inherited this place when my grandfather died two years ago."

"I'm sorry for your loss," Craig said. "I'm sorry that I didn't have an opportunity to meet him."

"Thank you. It's still hard to believe he's gone sometimes. My grandfather was born here in Connecticut. After my grandmother died, he left California and came back here to live and tend to the graves, just as his father had. It's been tended by family since the Civil War. My father and mother still live out West. I doubt anyone knows much more than I do, which obviously is nothing in regard to your grandfather."

Craig looked at her deep blue eyes as they studied the serene graveyard. He followed her gaze to the headstones and purple and white blooms growing every few feet. The place looked well-manicured and he thought that in spring and summer months, it must have taken her a few hours each week to mow the grass alone.

"You live here by yourself?" he asked.

Nell adjusted her attention from the small cemetery to Craig's face. "Yes. And where do you call home?"

Running his hand through his wind-blown hair, Craig smiled. "Well, I was born in Connecticut, but my folks moved to California when I was one. I was there until after college, then in the service for a few years. So I guess I don't have a place to call *home* yet. But Connecticut looks pretty appealing."

"That's weird that we both have families in California." Nell stepped aside indicating that he was invited to enter. "Would you like a cold drink before I show you to your grandfather?"

Craig took a few steps forward then waited while Nell closed the door before leading him to the square, old-fashioned kitchen. His eyes took in the fieldstone fireplace as they passed through the parlor, the vibrant colors in the Persian rugs. "Do you have coffee by any chance?"

"Hot coffee?"

Craig gave her a boyish grin. "I know, hot coffee on a hot day is not the usual."

Nell moved to a cupboard and placed a mug on the marble-topped kitchen island. "You're in luck. I made a pot this morning while it was still cool outside. I'll heat some for you. Milk and sugar?"

"Just black, thank you."

"Sit anywhere you'd like," Nell invited.

Craig stepped forward, pulled a seat out from the island, and watched as Nell poured coffee into his mug and heated it in her microwave. "So, what do you do with yourself out here? This place seems fairly isolated."

4

Nell ran cold water into a glass for herself. "I keep busy. Three days a week I work for a local veterinarian as a vet tech. The other four days are mine – I paint a little, watercolors, and I tend to the graves. It's peaceful – I like it here."

Craig studied her beautiful face, bright eyes, and middle-of-her-back length of hair the color of corn silk. Unbelievable, he thought, to find this much charm in a little cottage by a graveyard. "So, no more California for you?"

"This is it for me," she said with a faint smile. "Two years here, but I was hooked from the first moment I arrived. New England has everything – mountains, the sea, and a home-town atmosphere. I can walk to the town center for fresh fruit, home baked bread, and a good cup of coffee or tea, and sometimes an ice cream cone. The local people are very friendly – though some of them keep trying to marry me off to their grandsons or distant nephews."

Craig laughed. "I know the feeling." He beckoned to a closed door and a space he could see from the kitchen window. "So, the room at the back of the house, what's that, a dining room?"

Nell stiffened. "No, it's just kind of a mess, filled with old furniture and things like that."

He noticed her blush and thought about making a joke suggesting that she hid dead bodies out there. Instead he sipped his coffee and chose to be quiet.

5

"When you're ready, we'll take a walk out to your grandfather's grave. I have white daisies on the men's graves, purple violets for the ladies. I change it around from season to season."

Craig smiled. This girl was a rare find.

Minutes later they were walking through manicured lawns and grave markers of every description. Nell pointed out seven from the Civil War era. The most recent plot was her grandfather's, a grey granite rectangle engraved with his full name and a quote: *With gratefulness, from life to eternity.*

"It seems your grandfather was a man inspired by a simple life."

Nell nodded. "That's how he was. When he came back here to tend the graveyard many years ago, he still made time to visit us in California. This was really his home, while California was home to my grandmother. It was hard for him when she died in an accident several years ago."

They walked another twenty feet to the grave of Vincent William McGann, Craig's grandfather. Craig stopped to read the simple engraving, the name and dates of birth and death, nothing more. And then he bent to trace the name and to brush his fingertips to the cluster of white daisies. Standing after a moment, he looked around at the distant hills and the batch of pines guarding the west side of the graveyard. "This is an amazing place. I can see why Granddad wanted to be here, and to be near his good friend, *your* grandfather."

Nell squinted against the blazing sun and pushed her hair away from her neck and face. "It's coincidental that they both hailed from the west after years there. and that they died just a little less than two years apart. Friends forever."

Craig looked at Nell and thought he'd never seen a more beautiful woman in his life. He started to say something, but there was nothing to say except thank you for allowing him to visit the grave. "I should let you get back to whatever you were doing when I interrupted this morning. Thank you for the coffee. It hit the spot."

They turned and walked toward the cottage and Craig's dark blue sedan. They shook hands and parted, each wondering what had just happened.

Nell headed toward her cottage then stopped to pull a few weeds near the front door before walking to the kitchen for a glass of cold water. She stood staring out through the window over the sink, the view spectacular of the Berkshires. She thought about Craig, his gentle nature, his considerably good looks. She smiled at herself then unlocked the back room and went inside where it was darkened and cool. It had startled her when Craig had inquired about what the space was about.

"Well, you guys," she began, "we nearly got caught. Never mind. All is well. I'll get you some fresh water, sunflower seed, and I found you a bunch of acorns first thing this morning. It's a feast. And today, Dennis, you've finished with your two weeks of meds. Posey and Daniel, sorry you two. You each need a dose for three more days. And, by the way, thank you for being quiet while my guest was here."

Nell took their plastic bottles to the kitchen and rinsed them out before filling them. She returned to the three young squirrels in separate cages, distributing medicine, food, and water. Each a victim of mother abandonment, fallen nest, or predator, but they were doing well. While pleased that she could help them, the concern was being discovered. She was not licensed to care for wild creatures, even though she'd saved many small animals while living in California. She knew that if the authorities found her small charges, they would likely seize, and possibly euthanize, them.

Leaving them to rest with a CD player as low as it could go, she decided that listening to the gentle tones of Ravel's "Bolero" would be soothing to them – after all, even plants liked music. She opened one small window to invite in a soft breeze then quietly left the room, closing the door as she entered the kitchen.

It was nearly eleven o'clock when Nell changed her clothes and headed out to Bellwyn Animal Clinic. There she would treat animals in need, everything from rabbits, guinea pigs, dogs, and cats to the occasional pet rat or mouse. No matter the species, they were innocent little lives and Nell was always enthusiastic about saving them. The squirrels in her back room were her secret. She thought the environmental police were hard-nosed bullies. When Craig showed up at her door hours earlier, Nell had shuddered with fear that she'd been discovered. Thankfully, he was innocent and actually pretty nice. She wondered if she'd ever see him again.

Chapter Two

By the end of her day at work it was past eight and the light summer sky was beginning to settle into the lush branches of oaks, maples, and varieties of pines.

Nell was invigorated driving the three miles home where she would tend her little patients before taking a cool shower and settling down to a simple meal. Tomorrow she would be a nurse to her own, then she would paint. She smiled at the turn her life had taken, from good wages and fulltime nurse at a large animal hospital near Pasadena to a simple little clinic in Connecticut. The money was nowhere near the same, yet she had a free lodging and an existence she loved. At twenty-seven, Nell understood the integrity of this life, tending to family graves and little patients who needed help to survive. Money didn't need to fit into this equation.

With her freshly washed hair hanging loose about her shoulders, Nell pulled on a pair of tan colored shorts and a pink shirt. She rolled the sleeves to just below her elbows and walked into the kitchen where she selected a white Pane bread to toast. From her refrigerator she took cottage cheese and a large leaf of lettuce, then sat down to consume a sandwich and homemade lemonade. Just as she was about to take a bite, there was a knock at the front door.

Nell felt the familiar surge of adrenalin, always fearful of the squirrels being taken away. Who was out at nearly nine in the dark tapping on her door? No one from town ever came to visit.

She slid her stool back from the island and walked toward the door, asking who it was before she unhooked the latch.

"It's Craig," the voice replied. "I came by earlier but your car was gone. I have something I was hoping we could leave at my grandfather's grave."

Nell took a deep breath, pulled at her uncombed damp hair, then opened the door. Craig looked at her from head to bare toes then back to her luminous face. "Sorry to bother you. I know it's late."

Nell stepped aside. "No, it's okay. Come in. I was just having a bit of supper. Can I offer you something?" She turned and walked toward the kitchen, Craig following after closing the door.

"Thanks, but I had pizza in town. I wouldn't mind a cold drink though. What's that in your glass?"

Nell looked at the pale yellow liquid she had not yet touched. "Lemonade. Here, you have this. It's untouched, I'll pour more for myself. So, what do you have for your grandfather's grave?"

Craig pulled a stool away from the island and sat

down as he reached into his pocket pulling a white stone into his left palm. "This was part of a collection my grandparents had. They didn't buy souvenirs when they went on vacation trips. They brought home small stones, like this one. I've had this in my car since I left California – I'd like to tuck it in near the daisies if you don't mind."

Nell sat down with her glass of lemonade and took a sip as she reached for the smooth stone. "What a nice idea. It's dark out there now, and it's not unusual for a black bear to wander by. But if you want to place it on the grave tonight, we can take a flashlight and prepare to run, just in case."

Craig smiled. "You're kidding, right?"

Nell took a bite from her sandwich and shook her head from side to side. "Not kidding."

Craig's expression changed, his smile faded to perfectly formed lips.

Nell laughed and put her sandwich down. "There are bears here, along with a variety of other animals, but to tell you the truth, I haven't seen more than a few deer, a porcupine, birds, and squirrels since I arrived."

Craig drank half of his lemonade then gave Nell an intense look. "Maybe we should wait until morning. I can come back if that's okay."

Again she laughed. "That might be the better idea. Honestly, I've never been out in the dark since I came here. During the winter months I make sure there's wood for the fireplace right by the back door – I haven't thought to venture out to the shed at night. I have these suspicions that little critters might camp out in there to escape our typical snows."

Craig looked at her with interest. "You know, I'm not trying to suggest that there's danger in a woman living here alone, but isn't there? I mean, what if a storm required you to go outside to secure something – a wheelbarrow, shovels, repair a broken window?"

Nell sipped her lemonade then placed it down on the island. "Do you think a bear would prefer the taste of a woman over a man?"

Craig looked at her in astonishment then laughed.

Nell smiled at him again. "Craig, I haven't gone outside in the dark once. I have friends in town if something went terribly wrong. The fire department is noted to be very kind at rescuing cats from trees, boarding up broken windows for a temporary fix, and they even bandage your hand when you've managed to cut it on a fence wire."

"Did that happen to you?"

Nell nodded. "When I first moved in I was trying to repair a section near the shed. I caught my sleeve on the post and then my hand on the wire. I drove to the fire station and was promptly met by a medic who cleaned and bandaged the two-inch gash. I had a tetanus shot at Doctor Hemming's office that evening, and all was well. I feel very looked after here."

Craig shook his head. "But you have no close neighbors."

Nell shifted on her seat. "I own more than sixty acres. The other neighbors nearest to me also own large acreage – I have no problem with that."

Craig stood and looked out into the dark through the kitchen window. "It's a great place, but the last thing I thought I'd find here is a young woman living on her own. You were a surprise to me."

Nell nodded. "I kind of get that."

"Would you mind," he asked as he turned to face her, "if I come back in the morning? Are you working tomorrow?"

Nell stood and finished her lemonade before rinsing out the glass. "I'm here tomorrow; if you'd like to come by with the stone, that would be fine."

Craig rose and took his glass to the sink near to where Nell was. He tried hard not to take in every inch of her in those tan shorts with even darker tanned legs. "Great. It's getting late. I'll let you settle in for the night and see you in the morning then."

Nell ran water into his glass then walked with him to the front door. "What do you do for a living anyway? Is there a job waiting for you back in California?"

Craig turned to face her at the front door. "I've decided to stay in Connecticut for a while. I have computer work I can do – when I got out of the military, I reconnected with a company I'd interned at during college. My other experience is with the National Animal Protective Services. It's a decent organization, so I may see if they have any openings."

Nell froze. She knew of that group from California, similar to the New England version of wildlife police.

"Are you okay? You just went very pale."

Nell swallowed and looked down at her bare feet before looking briefly up at Craig. "No, no, it's just that you surprised me with the idea of staying here in Connecticut – you caught me off guard. What did you do with NAPS?"

Craig smiled. "Ah, being from California you recognize that organization. I was on the rescue team, kind of the police for animals. They have no voice; those of us on the team protect them."

Nell looked away as she opened the front door. "Sometimes."

Craig looked at her quizzically. "You disapprove of NAPS?"

Nell stepped aside so that he could walk past her to the outside. "I heard of times when they were off track, bullies. Not everyone who takes care of wildlife is doing a bad job. Some are the only hope wildlife has."

Craig was quiet as he studied her face. "I can respect your opinion. I suppose wrong is done, but when I was on the team, we saved many from mishandling. There was an instance where a man kept a raccoon as a pet in a cage where the poor animal could barely turn around."

Nell understood and accepted that was wrong for the animal. "What did you do with that raccoon?"

"The raccoon went to a sanctuary where he went through a year's adaption before he was released into a safe, natural environment."

Nell was quiet. She'd heard other stories.

"That's a happy ending that doesn't always happen. I understand your concern, especially since you work for a vet, but it was sometimes necessary to do what was conceived as best for the animals."

When Nell was quiet and had looked away from him, Craig realized it was time to go. "So, is tomorrow around nine okay?"

"Sure," she said as he stepped outside, then she closed the door. Once she heard the motor of his car, Nell stepped back and gasped at the thought of him ever discovering her tiny patients. If he decided to join NAPS in the New England area, she was going to avoid him like the plague, no matter how attractive he was. *Damn, I meet someone I feel vibes for and he turns out to be the enemy.*

After he'd pulled away from her cottage, Nell walked back to check on the squirrels. She closed the window to night air and spoke softly to them as she said goodnight and went in to sit near the hearth. She switched on TV and stared at the screen, her mind fastened on the fear invoked due to Craig's former position with NAPS. She detested that organization. The stories she'd heard about them were not good. Not every rescued animal was kept in a cage too small, and not every rescue was taken to a sanctuary either. She muted the TV and picked up a book to read, but she couldn't concentrate. He was returning in the morning to place the stone on his grandfather's grave, but most troubling was his decision to remain in Connecticut. It was a big state. She hoped he'd find a place to live and work a good distance away. If she never saw him again, it would be fine with her.

Up at six the next morning, the birds chirping and the sun glistening through the nearby willow, Nell changed from a pair of lightweight pajamas to pale blue jeans and a long shirt almost to her knees. She brushed her hair, washed her face, and went first to the squirrels. Medicine was given to two, food and fresh water to all three. Nell added small clumps of timothy hay to their cage floors and then opened a window for refreshing early day air.

Once they were settled, she decided to make a small batch of waffles on her grandfather's old iron. She had promised herself fresh pineapple, but that could be lunch. She mixed the batter and heated the waffle iron, spreading a small amount of butter on its grill. While the waffle cooked, she heated maple syrup, the real kind, and then made a pot of coffee.

Looking through her kitchen window, she marveled at the green-gold meadows and the occasional burst of color from wild blooms as far as she could see. There had been house upon house where she'd lived in California, neighbors on every side. Living in her cottage surrounded by nature suited Nell. She loved the tranquility and ability to take care of small animals, which her parents would not have been pleased with. They liked their pets – a dog, a cat – but according to some others wild animals were supposed to survive on their own. Nell wondered what had made her different from her family, what had been automatically instilled in her even as a child? Everything, she thought, needs a little help now and then.

At just around nine she heard Craig's car, and this time she didn't wait for him to come to the door. She walked outside as he shut off the motor. He stepped out of the car and smiled. She melted but composed herself quickly, reminding herself that he was the opposition.

"Hi," he said. "What a gorgeous day, huh?"

"Yes, it is," Nell said as she walked toward him.

After glancing at her summery attire and golden locks, Craig cocked his head and said, "Do I smell pancakes?"

Nell held her breath for a moment then murmured, "Waffles."

She had batter left but decided it was far too risky to

invite him in. If he were in almost any other profession, she'd have offered waffles and coffee.

Craig smiled and nodded as Nell suggested they head toward his grandfather's grave.

"You sure have a nice life here. Every time I drive up to this cottage, I feel like I'm in an enchanted village. Even the town center has those quaint qualities, an old-fashioned atmosphere. I can see why you love it here."

"Have you done anything about finding work?" Nell asked as they walked through the graveyard grass moist with morning dew.

"Nothing other than the computer analysis work I can do, but that's something I can work on wherever I land. All I know at this point is that this is where I want to settle."

Nell squinted against the morning sun. "Here? You mean in Keltonville?" Her stomach felt tied in knots.

"Yeah, if possible. I'm staying at the Yellow Brick Inn right now, but the owners, Joe and Mary Hale, they're going to ask a friend of theirs if an apartment they had for rent is still available. If it works out and I really like living here, I just might buy a house after a while."

Nell's nerves rippled with fear. This was not going to be a friendship, or any sort of relationship she could endure. Craig was a threat to her most basic need to empathize with wildlife. No man was good enough to shake her belief in caring for the innocents.

Reaching the headstone for Vincent McGann, they stood and looked down at the engraved name as if it had changed. Craig knelt and placed the small stone just beneath the soil of the white daisies. When he stood, Nell could see that his eyes were moist. The gesture was thoughtful, one that brought another element to who he was. It felt wrong to shun him, but she had no choice.

They remained silent for a few moments before Nell took a step backward and Craig turned to face her. "Thank you," he said. "I suppose it seems like a small gesture, but knowing how my grandparents coveted those little stones, it meant a lot to me to be able to leave one with Granddad for all time."

Nell nodded. "I think it was a perfect tribute."

They walked slowly back toward the cottage, Nell feeling a little guilty not inviting Craig in for coffee, but it was more risk than she was willing to take. If he even heard the squirrels, which once in a while she did from her kitchen, it could mean being reported and her small patients taken.

At her front door they stopped. Craig looked at her and then off toward the hills. "It's a beautiful place," he said. "I hope it will be okay for me to visit the graveyard from time to time."

"Yes, of course."

The stillness between them was awkward. "So, this

is your day off?"

Nell fussed with patting down a clump of grass then looked briefly up at Craig. "Yes, I'm not at the clinic for two days straight. I have a list of chores to do around here, and I may paint later. We'll see."

"Anything I can help you with?"

Nell took a breath before responding. He was so nice that it felt wrong to push him away. "Thanks, but I'm pretty well set, nothing heavy or complicated."

Craig seemed hesitant to leave but, after a moment of silence between them, he took the hint and thanked her. "Have a good day," he said as he walked toward his car. Within moments he was gone.

Nell stood on her steps watching him go and felt a pang of loneliness. It was unfortunate that he might pose a threat to her aiding animals in need. That sort of relationship simply would not work for her, not ever.

Chapter Three

After a day of watering thirsty grave flowers and painting a small meadow scene, Nell washed her brushes and took a glass of lemonade outside to her front door bench. She made a note that a coat of linseed oil might be in order since the bench was looking parched from daily morning sun. While she wasn't sure, she pictured her grandfather sitting there, taking in similar views.

Nell sat down, took a long drink, then balanced the glass against one crossed knee, her eyes on the distant hills and a weeping willow to her left. The place had been nurtured by a man who loved his years there, as had been done by others before him. Now it was her turn to keep the graves respectfully pleasing all while loving the task. How much better, she wondered, could life be? And then she thought of Craig. If only.

As she sat with her eyes closed, enjoying a gentle afternoon breeze against her bronzed skin, Nell heard a car engine coming close and saw that it was Craig. She stiffened with seeing him pull into her half circle gravel driveway and pull the car to a stop. Out of his car and walking toward her he smiled. "I was going by and couldn't resist stopping when I saw you sitting there. How are things?"

"Everything's fine. This road, although never particularly active, is one of the main leads into town. It's not unusual for people I know to wave to me or honk their horn."

Craig walked a bit closer. "Have you been enjoying your day off?"

"Yes, always." She hesitated then pushed to one side of the bench and asked, "Would you like lemonade?" .

"I'd love it if it's no trouble. Would you like me to fetch it? I know my way to your kitchen."

"No, no," she replied almost too quickly. "Sit down. I'll be right back."

Nell disappeared into the house and returned a couple of minutes later with a glass of lemonade for Craig. When she placed it in his left hand, their fingers touched, and she felt a chill.

"So, what have you been up to?" he asked. "Some fun I hope."

Nell nodded as she sat down inches from him. "Yes, I painted, and I watered the graveyard flowers. It was all relaxing. What about you?"

Craig leaned forward, his elbows on his knees, the glass of lemonade half consumed in his hands. "I had a good day, too. I'm getting that apartment I told about. It's in town over the bakery, three rooms and a nice bathroom with a giant shower. There's a deck off the back, really a perfect place for the time being."

Nell smiled. "You'll have the benefit of smelling that wonderful bread that Grace bakes. I find that place irresistible."

Craig looked at her and smiled. "Good, you can stop by to visit me."

Nell thought that probably wouldn't happen, but she said nothing to indicate her feelings. "So for now you have computer work you can do, right?"

"Yes. I actually talked with my employer in California today. They have an employee who resigned to teach, so there's mountains of work for me. It's perfect. I can make my own hours and what I need to do isn't stressful. Everything here is coming along well, just like it was meant to be."

Nell took a sip of her drink and wondered if she was happy or not. As much as she found Craig attractive beyond her wildest imagination, she feared what differences they could have and knew she had to keep him away from her squirrels.

"So," Craig said, "anything interesting going on in your animal world?"

Nell choked on her lemonade and set the glass down on the ground. "My animal world?"

Craig smiled at her and said, "Well, yes. At the clinic. You don't have any pets, right?"

Nell cleared her throat. "Not really. I mean, not yet.

24

I may adopt a cat soon. One of our clients is an elderly woman who may be leaving her home to live with a daughter. If that happens, she can't take her cat. I've offered to give him a home if necessary. It's up in the air at this point."

Craig finished his drink. "You have a nice life. This cottage is a great little place, and you're doing what you care about – taking care of animals, the graveyard, and painting. That's all cool stuff."

"Yes, it is. I like helping animals recover from an illness or a surgery. I gave fluids to three cats and two dogs yesterday, and I bandaged one cat's ear torn by a nail on a fence. It's rewarding."

"No bears, huh?"

Nell laughed. "Not yet."

"What other creatures do you repair? Any rabbits?"

Nell took a deep breath and nodded. "Sure, rabbits, guinea pigs, hamsters, rats..."

"Rats, really?"

"Sure, they're smart and lots of people, including me, love them."

Craig laughed. "I get the feeling you love *everything*," he said. "Although maybe bears are the exception."

Nell felt the smile spreading across her lips. "You were right the first time, *everything* that needs help. Dr. Hill would have to knock the bear out cold for me to work on it, but sure, I'd take care of a bear. When I was younger, I used to watch reruns of *Grizzly Adams*, and I fell in love."

Craig laughed then stood and thanked Nell for the lemonade as he handed her the glass. "So, since this is your day off, and you've been very hospitable to me, how about if I treat you to dinner out tonight? We could go for Italian, Chinese, whatever you choose."

Nell thought about the last time she'd been out to dinner with someone – it had been in California with Dave Whitten. That had been the most lackluster evening she could recall. She remembered him talking all evening about his work as a civil engineer. Full of himself, he never inquired about what Nell did for a living or what she liked to do for fun. When he called again for a second date, she told him she was busy.

Nell looked at Craig. "I don't think so, but thank you."

Craig looked a bit injured. "Oh. Do you already have plans?"

"Yes," she lied. "I'm sorry."

"Oh, don't be sorry. I guess I should have known you'd have someone you're seeing. Young, single, smart, and pretty. Why wouldn't you?"

Nell blushed and looked down as she stood. "It's nice of you to ask me to dinner. And I wish you luck in your new apartment and work. Sounds like everything is coming together for you. Welcome to Keltonville."

Craig hesitated as he studied her beautiful face then

turned and walked toward his car. "If it's okay," he began as he reached for the car door handle, "I'll come by again to visit the grave. There's something soothing about this space. I like knowing my grandfather is here."

Nell nodded then balanced their glasses in her left hand. "You're welcome to visit the grave whenever you wish. I'm guessing at this point you can find your way to it, so you don't even need to stop by the house first. See you later." She turned and walked inside the cool dwelling then stood at her kitchen sink, staring out to the meadows. Yes, it was beautiful, but it was also lonely, and then she realized that emotion had escaped her until she met Craig McGann. If only he weren't so handsome, so sweet, so smart, so everything.

She washed the two glasses then checked on the young squirrels. They were so dear, curled on their sides with their long tails wrapped around their bodies. She stood watching them for a few moments before tiptoeing out of the darkened room to her kitchen. Wouldn't it be nice if she could have it all? she thought. Taking care of these little ones and Craig at her side. It seemed he was bound to be back frequently to visit his grandfather's grave. There was an element of comfort in that thought, as well as a portion of fear.

After a day filled with satisfaction, Nell sat down after dark by her hearth and made a list of items she needed in town. She would go tomorrow for basics at the small grocery store, and maybe she'd stop at the bakery for a loaf of rye. Then she remembered that Craig lived above the bakery now. Maybe she'd skip the bread. When the list was made, Nell picked up her book, removed the bookmark, and began to read. Settling back into the large chair, she reached above her to the floor lamp and adjusted the light from dim to bright. Everything about this house was comfortable. Her grandfather had been efficient in how he lived, keeping everything simple yet convenient. What she knew was that this was home, forever.

Thinking about Craig brought a smile. He was irresistible in looks and personality, yet potentially perilous to the welfare of her little charges. Their lives mattered more than a flirtatious interest in Craig McGann. Her intention was to keep him at bay.

With the book in her lap, her hands folded on its cover, she fell asleep. Shifting her position in the chair, Nell woke herself with the movement. She realized that the night air in the Berkshires could sweep in with darkness and cool the house enough to warrant a blanket in bed. She stood, left the book where she'd been sitting, shut out all but one light, and went to her room.

With morning sun filtering through old lace curtains, Nell went first to check on the squirrels. She smiled at their energetic movements and watched as they nibbled on acorns and hazelnuts, a favorite combination for each one of them. They had full water bottles, and their cages were clean. She decided to deliver medicine to Daniel and Posey *after* making coffee and getting dressed.

Stopping at the clinic on the way into town, Nell pulled up to a front space, turned the car's engine off, and walked into the small lobby. Lorna, the desk attendant, was there with a ready smile for Nell. "What are you doing in here today? Aren't you off?"

Nell smiled. "Yes, I am, but I was wondering if Doctor Hill was busy just now. I'd like to steal a minute from him."

Lorna looked at Nell's fresh young face and nodded. "You know he'll make time to see you. You're his pet." They both laughed as Lorna turned, knocked gently on the doctor's office, and informed him that Nell would like to speak with him.

"You're out and about early," he said as he smiled at his young assistant. "What have you got hidden in your house now?"

Nell smiled and walked to a cabinet where medical supplies were kept. "I was wondering if you think I should stop or continue with the meds for two of my patients. They seem to be doing well, but I always worry that I'm cutting them short."

Doctor Hill glanced up at the clock on his wall then nodded at Nell. "You always worry when you're about through with the medicine routine. Are they sneezing? What I gave you should have been enough, but if you're nervous, you can take a little more and do an extra day or two. You know more about squirrels than I do, Nell. What do you think?"

Nell squirmed. "They seem well. They're eating and playing. I guess we're safe."

He put a finger to his lips and winked. "Mum's the word. We're safe as long as we don't get caught, but there's little chance of that at your secluded cottage. Take some extra meds with you if you want. Better safe than sorry."

Nell reached into the cupboard for some more of the antibiotics that would be delivered in small tubes to the little mouths. It was something she'd done several times since moving to Connecticut, each patient surviving and being released out into her shed where they could scamper to trees as they wished. This was the first time she'd had three at the same time.

Nell had a passion for wildlife. They didn't have an easy existence between cold weather and predators. If she took Mrs. Olden's cat eventually, that cat would be staying indoors, away from unsuspecting birds and other small creatures. It simply wasn't fair to allow a well-fed pet to frighten and possibly end the life of a squirrel, chipmunk, mouse, or bird.

Leaving the clinic, Nell stopped at the grocers for a few simple items and then looked across the street toward the bakery. She wanted that rye bread, but she also saw Craig's car parked next to the small building and decided it would be risky. She was going to do everything possible to discourage their friendship.

As she opened her car door, she heard her name being called and knew it was Craig. She turned to look toward the bakery and saw that he was upstairs, his window open, his right hand waving to her.

"Come see my digs," he said with a smile. "I bet you're coming here for bread anyway. I'll even make you some coffee."

Nell closed her car door after leaving two small bags in the back seat. She hesitated then walked across toward the bakery. The door to the left of the shop's entrance was opened and Craig stood there wearing jeans and no shirt. She was stunned with his bare chest, and it showed on her face.

"Come on up," he gestured toward the stairway. "I'll pull a shirt on and make that coffee."

"Oh," she said as she reached the top step, "don't make coffee unless you want it. I've had mine for the morning. I really need to get my groceries home." Her eyes canvassed the small space, a fan blowing cool air into the room.

Craig slipped his arms into a pale blue shirt and buttoned it nearly to the top. "What do you think? It's not bad, huh? A bedroom, bathroom, kitchenette, and a living room. Plenty of space for the time being."

Nell liked the layout. It was comfortable and the view of town was perfect. "It's nice. Did it come furnished?"

Craig smiled. "It did."

"You seem to have settled in very quickly."

"When things feel right, there's no reason to hesitate. It worked out perfectly for me since I had nothing but my clothing and my computer and Grace didn't have anyone living here. I figured there was no point in continuing to stay at the inn."

She nodded and considered that perhaps this was a man who didn't hesitate in life – just jumped in with both feet, who saw what he wanted and grasped it. At the same time, she understood as she'd felt very much the same when she first arrived at the cottage. There was no question about whether it would become her home. As soon as she was there, it was.

"So, I was wondering about us getting together for dinner tonight. I passed by a nice looking restaurant just outside of town. Do you like Italian food?"

Nell felt caught. "Um, yes, but probably not tonight."

Craig looked at her with a quizzical expression. "You have plans for tonight?"

Nell took a deep breath. "No, not really. I just have things I had thought I might do with it being my day off and all."

Craig put his hands on his hips and studied her

beautiful face. He wanted to ask if she didn't like him but instead he was awkwardly quiet. Nell picked up on the atmosphere and felt guilt as well as regret for her quick refusal. Being with him was just too precarious. Damn NAPS for having been part of his former life. What would he reveal if he knew about her squirrels?

Craig sat down on the arm of his sofa and looked at her. "Is there ever going to be a good time for us to have dinner together? Are you seeing someone? I mean, I don't want to make it difficult for you if I'm getting in the way. But you're the only person here I really know. And it would be nice to not have to eat alone."

Nell swallowed again and looked around the room. "No, I'm not involved with anyone, but that's sort of the way I want it." She looked at his face and seeing his serious expression she continued. "It's just that I have a lot going on between work and the cemetery and keeping up with the house and my painting. I haven't really thought much about dating."

Craig looked at her for a long few moments then smiled softly. "Okay, let's not call it a date. Do you think you could fit me into your life long enough to consume a meal?"

Nell squirmed. "I suppose so. Okay, so tonight around seven. Right now I need to get my groceries home. I like your apartment – thanks for having me up. It's certainly close to the grocery store, very convenient."

Craig stood and looked at her. "I'll pick you up at seven."

Nell wondered if she could take a step. Her heart was pounding at the prospect of spending time with him. "Okay," she said as she slowly moved toward the stairs and then outside.

Across the street and in her car, she turned the key. With the air conditioning set on high, she pulled away toward her home wondering what she was getting herself into.

Chapter Four

After unpacking her groceries, Nell checked in on the squirrels then left the extra meds from Dr. Hill in a small cupboard. The air in that room was cool and refreshing, her little patients each looking well as they nibbled on sunflower seed and acorns. She smiled at the mess they made. They weren't the neatest little creatures she'd ever known.

In her kitchen Nell put her food items away and then poured herself a cold glass of water and took it into the living room where she moved her book from the night before and sat down. Somewhat mad at herself for caving in to Craig's invitation, she had to figure out a plan to avoid letting him get too close.

In another world where she didn't have concern for her tiny patients, Nell would have been elated with the invitation to dinner from someone as remarkable and charming as Craig. If only it he hadn't been involved with NAPS. She understood from her head to her toes that this evening out was going to have to be the last. She needed to nip this intrusion into her life before it became more cohesive than it already was. In just a few short days, he had made himself part of her life.

Having emptied her glass of water to the last sip, Nell set it on a coaster and then went to look through her closet to figure out what to wear to a nice Italian restaurant with a handsome escort. She looked at a knee-length skirt in white and a black blouse with white polka dots. No. The skirt was too short. She took a hanger holding a purple dress with a full skirt and held it against herself. No, too fancy. Her eyes scanned the closet and stopped at a cornflower blue dress with sleeves to the elbow, the length just below her knees. That with tan sandals would do, a relaxed look as though she hadn't put much thought into attire for their first and last evening out.

It was after noon when Nell decided to water the flowers at the seventy-four graves. She hesitated at her grandfather's gravestone and wished she'd had more time with him. Everything in the cottage reflected who he was. The comfort, the charm, the colors of rugs and furniture were all his doing, and he'd done it well. There was almost nothing she wished to change except for little things, like new curtains in her bedroom, a new quilt for the bed, then a few nice mugs for the kitchen and one small frying pan. Thinking she had more than she required in that two-bedroom cottage, Nell smiled at the arrangement of furniture, the items he'd selected when moving in. Some of the older pieces, she'd been informed, had been removed when he arrived from California. A few pieces, including the bedding, had been taken away.

Having watered the flowers at each grave, Nell walked to a rose bush where pale blooms flourished. She leaned in to enjoy their sweet aroma then decided to take a few stems into the house to enjoy at the kitchen island. With the fresh bouquet before her, Nell made half a sandwich with fresh tomatoes and mayonnaise then sat down with lemonade to enjoy her lunch. As she swallowed, she remembered she had a date at seven and her mouth seemed suddenly dry. *Why did I allow this to happen?*

Having washed her small plate and glass, she walked to the drawer in the kitchen where she kept her stash of paints and removed an eight by ten inch piece of watercolor paper. She sat back down at the island and began to lightly sketch the blush-colored roses. They were delicate in color as well as in fragrance, such beautiful gifts.

Nell wondered who had planted them. They weren't wild, but there were multiple bushes and they were older plantings. Everything – the house, the graves, the hills in the distance – at this piece of land was absolutely perfect. She thought back to her childhood in the Pasadena area, and as beautiful as it was, there was no chance for this much privacy and everyday charm. She understood that her parents preferred a more cultivated atmosphere. Even as a child, Nell preferred trees and wildflowers over next-door neighbors. She wondered if she'd been considered unsociable. Maybe, at least regarding humans.

By near to four in the afternoon her painting of pink roses was finished enough to set it aside. She heated herself a cup of morning coffee and stood leaning against the sink as she examined the fragile blooms she'd managed to capture on the piece. That, she thought, might be suitable for framing and sending to Mom for her birthday. One thing Nell loved about her parents was their pride in her creative ability. They wanted her to go to art school, but instead she trained to care for animals.

After a cool shower and pulling on a pair of shorts and a lightweight shirt, Nell walked around the cottage, checking to see if she should give dusting or vacuuming a consideration. Seeing her book, she decided all was well and that what she'd prefer to do was read. It was, after all, her day off.

At six-thirty, she stood, walked to her bedroom and brushed her long strands before slipping the blue dress over her head, smoothing the skirt. Looking in the mirror she decided it was perfect, not too dressy, not too casual. She slipped her feet into the sandals and then walked to the squirrel room where she freshened their water and gave them more hazelnuts. She laughed at their eagerness for the tasty little cache of food and then, just as she closed their door, there was a knock from the front of the house.

"Hi," he said as his eyes traveled from her blonde locks to her sandaled feet. "You look beautiful, as usual."

Nell could feel her cheeks warm and she backed away. "Just give me a minute to grab my purse." She moved to a coat rack where she lifted a pale shoulder bag onto her arm and then walked toward Craig with butterflies doing summersaults in her stomach.

His eyes appraised her again, and he determined that she was definitely worth a second lasting look.

Nell observed his khaki slacks and short-sleeved white shirt against muscular sun-kissed arms. He was absolutely too good looking. And those eyes. She wondered whether she just hadn't noticed the eyes of other men she'd known or if Craig McGann was truly outstanding. While his facial features weren't magazine model material, he had this demeanor about him that was appealing and reflected confidence. She doubted any woman would turn away if he entered the room – he was captivating.

Nell locked the door, then Craig reached for her hand, interlacing his fingers with hers. She was both unsettled and electrified at how natural it felt to allow his warm hand over hers. Some she had dated would not have been accepted had they claimed her in such a way. He led her around to the passenger door, opened it for her, and she slid inside. Once she was settled, he released her hand and shut the door then moved around the front to get in.

Craig fastened his seat belt and gave Nell another look. The blue dress beautifully accented her eyes. He couldn't figure out if she was gorgeous or cute or just knock-out stunning. He decided she was all three.

"Have you been to Leonardo's before?" he asked while pulling out of the driveway.

"No, I don't like to dine alone, so I prepare most of my own food."

Craig smiled. "You've been dining alone? Does this mean I have no competition?"

Nell stared out the window as they passed meadows and a cluster of pines. She glanced over toward him and wasn't sure how to reply. "I haven't dated since I moved here. I have friends at the clinic, but they're married. They go home to their husbands and wives at day's end."

Craig nodded, his confidence heightened by her proclamation of being available.

Within minutes they pulled into the restaurant parking lot. Nell unfastened her seatbelt and gathered her purse. As she reached for the handle, Craig was already there opening her door. She swung her legs to the right and stepped out of the car, taking his hand that was waiting to help her to her feet.

"I'm not sure I've ever paid much attention to this building before," she said. "It's nice, very homey, and it smells good even from outside."

"I was told that the food is excellent," Craig said as he drew her toward the door and inside. "And it was also advised to save room for the desserts, cannoli or rum slices. According to Grace, it's an irresistible conclusion to the meal."

Nell laughed. "And did she happen to also suggest something for a meal?"

He joined in her laughter as he held open the door. Once inside, they were greeted by the hostess who took them to a table by a hearth where a huge fern sat in place of a blazing fire.

Craig sat down across from her and glanced between her and the menu. "I'm not sure which to go for – their lasagna or the spaghetti with vegetarian meatballs."

Nell looked up from her menu to him. "You eat vegetarian meatballs?"

"Yup, ever since I went to work with NAPS. You save animals whenever possible, and eating them doesn't seem quite right." He smiled at her then looked back at the menu.

Nell was being won over. She had given up meat when she was somewhere near ten, much to her parents' disagreement. They worried she'd be lacking in nutrition, but Nell insisted that she could not consume anything with a face. Now here was this adorable man who didn't eat meat for the same reasoning. How did this happen? It seemed unfair that he was from her home state, he was a vegetarian, and he was sensational in looks. Some strange force was working against her, and then she thought of the squirrels. They would be released in another month, yet there would be others. Nothing was going to keep her from aiding them in their times of need. Not even a handsome young man.

Warm bread and butter placed before them their orders were taken. Nell chose the eggplant lasagna and so did Craig. Red wine was offered, and they each had one glass, the ruby red color adding to the festive evening.

"It's nice," Nell said after taking a sip. "I usually go for white wine, but this is light, and very pretty."

Craig smiled and touched his glass to hers. "From what I've observed, they come around with the wine a few times while dinner is being consumed. If you'd prefer white, I'm sure they have it."

"No," she said after taking another sip, "this is good, but thank you."

Craig swallowed a few sips as he took her in. "So, tell me about yourself."

Nell studied his face for a moment then shrugged her shoulders. "I'm not sure what else there is to tell. I came from California just like you. Our grandfathers were friends, and they're both buried in my cemetery. I work as a vet tech, and I paint. There's nothing else."

Craig looked at her and smiled. "I'd bet there are

things you haven't revealed."

Nell's stomach felt the current of adrenalin rushing through as she looked from his face to the large hearth. "No, not really."

"Well, why don't you tell me what you did today?"

Relieved to have something to focus on, Nell talked about how she'd spent her afternoon and early evening. Then she asked him about his day. It all felt natural, like it always was.

When their meals were served, Nell commented that there was enough on each plate for two people. Craig smiled. "I bet they'll give us a doggie bag if needed, but you might want to save a little room for one of those sweets."

Nell took a bite of the lasagna and closed her eyes. It was the best she'd ever had. When she opened her eyes Craig was smiling at her reaction as he pressed a napkin to his lips and reached for his wine.

"This is outrageously delectable," she said having swallowed the first bite.

Craig nodded. "This is certainly a contender for the best Italian food I've had in my life, and I've spent time in Italy. I'm glad you're enjoying it. Now aren't you glad you didn't find a reason not to go out with me tonight?"

Nell, not knowing what to say, simply smiled and put another bite of lasagna in her mouth.

"I'm glad you said yes to this evening. I think we

have a lot in common and we are, after all, going to be neighbors. Tell me about your name. I love the simplicity. It suits you."

She cut another bite of lasagna and responded, "There's not much of a story behind it. My mother had a favorite book she'd read when she was twelve. The main character was Nell."

He nodded and decided that she deserved her name, coming from a memorable character her mother favored. Craig watched her take the next bite of lasagna and knew that he would be happy to sit across from her every meal for the rest of his life.

"My middle name is a bit longer," she said after taking a long swallow of water. "It's Miranda."

Craig looked at her face and thought that her name, Nell Miranda McGann, was as beautiful as she deserved. This was a woman he didn't want to offend, a woman with whom he felt complete in her presence.

"I love that combination," he said. Then kiddingly he continued, "It's a good thing you won't have to change it when we get married."

Nell nearly choked on her own saliva. She looked from his handsome face to her food, her right hand in mid-air with a fork full of lasagna. She lowered the fork to her plate and was still.

He laughed a bit too loud, drawing attention from the other diners. "I'm just kidding," he reassured her. "Sometimes I need tape on my mouth. Really, please, enjoy your food. I'll be quiet."

Nell looked at him and wasn't sure of her next move. "Tell me something about you that I don't know. I already know your middle name is Vincent, for your grandfather."

Craig thought for a moment before answering. "Let me see...something you don't already know. Okay, I once had a pet raccoon."

She looked at him in surprise. "You did? This is a story I need to hear more about. How old were you? And how did you come across a raccoon?"

"I was in the car with my uncle, my father's brother. We saw a raccoon on the side of the road and pulled over to see if it could be saved. Unfortunately, it was a deceased mother, but there was a baby next to her. My uncle buried the mom off to the side and I scooped the little one into my uncle's jacket. We took him home. My mother showed me how to feed him, and they let me keep him in our screened porch."

"How long? I mean, could you pick him up? And what did your dad think?"

Craig reached for his water glass and took a few sips. "My parents were both okay with Teddy – yes, I named him Teddy. He lived on the porch for the better part of a year, then we opened the door and allowed him to go. He didn't go. He went outside, scratched around at a few things he found interesting on the ground, then he came back into the screened porch. At night we closed the door to keep him safe. Eventually he left the porch, but he always came back to visit. We had a lot of trees around us. He had the best of both worlds for several years."

Nell liked that Craig had been exposed to kindness toward wild animals. "So, how long did he stay, and what happened to him?"

"He stayed around our house for at least three years until he found himself a lady. They would come together for handouts, chirping their thanks for the offerings. By the time I was ready for college, Teddy was a rare sight in our yard. It seemed he'd fathered a few little ones and that he was having a great life. My parents saw him for a few years after I was gone, and then he stopped coming. We have no idea what became of him, but he had to have been ten or twelve when we last saw him."

Nell took another bite of her dinner then asked, "So what drove you into becoming part of NAPS? Did they know you had a raccoon as a boy?"

"Yeah, actually, when I decided to get involved with animal rights, I met a NAPS officer. He and I talked about Teddy and he thought it was great. He persuaded me to join the team, said they needed compassionate people on board."

"So you joined?"

"Not right away. I wanted to see for myself what they were about. At first I volunteered. Then I worked for them summers while I was in college. After that I went into the Army, but if I was back home, I'd probably be looking for work with NAPS. Some of what I saw was harsh, people who might have intended to be caretakers but who had animals like Teddy in cages too small and often filthy. If the animals don't have access to their natural habitat, it can be difficult to care for them – their nails get too long and can grow into their paws, or their teeth can get too long and they have trouble eating. Those animals had to be taken, rehabilitated, then released at various sanctuary sites. Or, sometimes, the most kind thing to do was to euthanize."

Nell shook her head. "I knew someone who worked as a rehabilitator. She told me of times when NAPS seized animals from people with good intentions. I grew up thinking of NAPS as the enemy."

"And you might have been right in some instances. Some of the people I worked with were pretty stark about taking wildlife away from being treated as pets. A few of those cases were right – the animals didn't have any sense of adventure being confined, but there were also times when animals like Teddy were very well cared for. Humanity is complex."

Nell reached for her water. "That's, perhaps, being too kind to humanity. I love wildlife. They have it hard trying to manage on what's available for food and living through tough weather conditions. It sounds like your Teddy had a good arrangement."

Craig nodded. "He did. He was free to come and go once he was old enough. I think about him a lot."

Nell took a few more bites of her food then sat back as the waiter took their plates to box for home. They ordered a mini tray of desserts and coffee then sat and managed to have a lighter conversation.

"Would you like to go for a ride?" he asked as they left the restaurant. "It's just a little before ten."

"I think," Nell began, "that since tomorrow is a work day, it would be best to call it an evening. I enjoyed dinner with you. Good food and good company are always appealing."

"So you'll agree to another time again soon?" he said as he opened her car door and she slid inside.

Nell smiled but didn't reply. He moved into position behind the steering wheel and started the engine. The ten-minute drive to her cottage was less communicative, a time of silence and reflection.

With the engine off and sitting before her front door, Craig looked at his beautiful passenger. Nell looked at him, and they both smiled at the same time. It was like being a teen on the first date, just a bit awkward.

"You didn't give me an answer," he said.

"To?"

"To another time together. Whatever you choose, whenever you choose. I enjoyed getting to know you better tonight."

Nell turned to look at her front door, the lights in the cottage were soft and inviting. She knew she would like more shared meals with him, but having the squirrels made that prospect impossible for now. "It was a very nice meal. Thank you."

Craig was quiet, not sure he'd won her heart. When she moved to open her car door, he opened his own and met her with a helping hand before walking her to the house. Nell inserted her key in the lock, opened the door, then turned to thank Craig for a lovely evening.

Despite a desperate desire to kiss her, he was not making a move. He nodded, watched her get inside and waited for her to lock the door. He knew this was a girl he had to tread softly with, no mistakes. As he walked to his car, he looked back to see if he could get one last glimpse of Nell.

Inside, she leaned against her door, not daring to watch him walk away. Afraid she wouldn't be able to stop herself from opening the door and inviting him in.

Chapter Five

Changing into a grey jersey set she could sleep in as well as wander around the house, Nell went to check on her squirrels. They were babies still, used to the warmth of their mothers' bodies in the nest. She closed the window to night air and opened each of the three cages to deliver a gentle stroke and a whisper of tenderness. There was more to survival and recovery than medicine and a safe space.

Having left the cornflower blue dress across her bed, Nell placed it on a hanger and smiled at the evening she'd enjoyed with Craig. If only, she thought, she could trust that he wasn't a danger.

Back in her kitchen she made tea and looked out at the night sky. Filled with radiant specks and moon-lit clouds, she felt a chill and hugged her arms close to her body. Everything before Craig had been orderly, her life simple, a chain of must dos and time to play. With him in her life, his lack of predictability, Nell was feeling both elated and disturbed.

She thought about his pet raccoon, Teddy, and she smiled. But then he joined NAPS which concerned her. What would he have felt if someone in a dark uniform had taken Teddy away? Despite not being licensed, Craig had obviously given the raccoon an opportunity to thrive. And while some might be careless with wildlife, there were others who saved them, who made their lives wonderful as well as worthwhile. There was too much grey area for these cases to be treated with a stark ruling that all wildlife needed to be removed and possibly destroyed. It was simply wrong to Nell. There weren't enough rehab people available – she believed others should be trained and accepted into the fold. Dr. Hill understood, she understood, many got it, that if a life could be saved and made better, why would anyone object?

When she sat down with her tea and the book she'd been reading, the phone rang. It was nearly eleven and she wondered who would be calling. She smiled as she looked at the phone and saw that it was her parents in California.

"Hey, Mom, how are things?"

"Well, to begin with, this is Dad," the voice on the other end of the line chided. "All is well here. How are you doing, honey buns."

Nell laughed. "I'm doing just fine. What have you and Mom been up to?"

"You know us – a little of this and a little of that. We took a little sentimental journey to Carmel last weekend, so beautiful there. But we're back and ready to pull weeds from the garden and mow the yard. It grows fast in a week. I'd bet you know all about that with the cemetery you care for."

"Yes, I do. But I love it. It's kind of a gift to the folks buried there to keep it nice. Anything new going on I should know about?"

"Not really. Your mother is busy with her garden club, and I'm going to be spending the day at Cleddon Beach this coming Saturday with my environmental pals, cleaning up as much debris as we can find. It's good exercise as well as a gift to the ocean."

Nell smiled. "I'm glad you do that. It's a worthy cause."

"I think," he said, "joining worthy causes runs in the family. You and the animals. I remember well how every injured bird came to our yard looking for you."

Nell laughed. "Now wait a minute. I didn't call to them or have a sign out."

"They knew," her father said. "So, anything else going on we should be aware of? We miss you, you know."

Nell thought for a moment. It occurred to her that she might mention Craig, but she decided there was no point in getting her father thinking about a potential budding romance that she wasn't sure if she even wanted. "I'm keeping busy. The clinic is always booked to capacity. Everyone loves Dr. Hill, and I like working there. Other than that, I've been keeping the graves looking nice, and, of course, I paint."

"We're proud of you, Nell. It doesn't keep us from missing you, but you've always been a good girl. I'm just sorry you love Connecticut so much."

Nell nodded. "I know. The distance isn't ideal, but you and Mom can come out anytime you'd like."

"Well, you know your mother doesn't like to fly, but you come here to visit when you can. That fellow, Dave Wicken, or Whitten, whatever his name is, he's asked for you when I've seen him in town. Seems like a nice enough fellow. What happened there?"

Nell raised her eyebrows and smiled. "Nothing. He just wasn't my type, and it just takes one out of two to ruin the mood. You and Mom have it right, but not everyone finds a good fit."

"And you haven't yet?"

Nell looked around at her cozy living room. "This house, this life, my work, is a good fit. But if you're wondering if I've found love, the answer is nope, not yet."

Her father laughed and said, "Well, when it feels right, it just happens."

"So I've heard," Nell replied, smiling at how coincidental that he'd use those same words Craig had said earlier that day.

They continued to talk, her father filling her in on the neighbors and his projects. When the call ended, Nell left her book on the chair and turned off lights as she made her way to the kitchen. She drank the last of

her tea then set the cup in the sink before heading for
sleep.

***

The morning sun poured into her room. Nell swung
her legs to the side of her bed and slipped her bare feet
into soft socks. Work was waiting, but first, the
squirrels. She gave Daniel and Posey their meds, fed
them all, opened a screened window, then dressed for
her job. With a cup of coffee in her hands she scurried
about the cottage raising shades, opening windows,
and giving one last check on the squirrels. All was well
at home. Now she was ready to mend little bodies at
Dr. Hill's side.

When she pulled into her driveway mid-afternoon,
Craig pulled in from the opposite direction, their cars
meeting nose to nose in the small circular space. Her
heart skipped beats seeing him, and she knew there
were two distinct reasons – she liked him and she
feared him.

"Hi there," he said as he stepped from his car and
walked toward her. "I was just going by and saw you
pulling in. How was your day?"

Nell closed her car door and waited until he was by
her side. "Everything went well. Where are you
coming from?"

"I actually went on a little errand for the bakery. I
went in this afternoon to buy a loaf of bread and they
were frantic over needing rye flour. I asked where they

54

bought it and it was just over in Bellowton. I offered to go get it for them so they could bake first thing tomorrow."

Nell gave him an approving smile. "That was nice of you. I especially like rye bread."

"Well then, I'm very glad to be of assistance. So, do you have plans for this evening? We could grab a bite to eat. After working on my computer all day, I'm feeling like I need a little diversion."

Nell cocked her head to one side. "I'm a diversion?"

Craig studied her face. Even in the dark blue uniform from the clinic, she was stunning. "Well, that's not *all* you are."

She hesitated. "While I don't have specific plans, I do have things to attend to."

"Will those *things* take all evening? I know a place where we could get a wonderful Greek salad and a margarita."

Nell laughed. "That's a combination, Greek and Mexican delights together."

"Ah, so you like the idea. You did say *delights*."

Nell smiled. "Are you thinking of Spring Brook Café?"

"Exactly," he said, his grin broadening. "You obviously know the place."

"I know their Greek salads. I love them."

"And their margaritas?"

"Haven't had one of those at Spring Brook. I

usually just get take-out. It's not my style to go into a restaurant to eat alone. Seems like you're getting very familiar with all of the local establishments though."

"Well, a single guy has to eat, right? So, what do you say? Greek salad and margaritas?"

"It's a daring combination., isn't it?"

"It's a *great* combination. You have to try it. Come on, make my evening."

Nell paused in thought before replying. "If you can give me an hour, I'll go with you."

"No problem. I'll take the flour to the bakery, get changed, and be back. It's fortuitous that I caught you pulling into your driveway. A few minutes earlier, and you wouldn't have been home, and a few minutes later, you'd have already been inside. I would have been hesitant to disturb you by knocking on your door."

"Yes, well, as they say, timing is everything. I'll write down my phone number and give it to you tonight – that way you'll have an option to call. See you in an hour." She watched as he backed out of the driveway as she headed inside, first to the squirrels then to the shower.

As she dried her hair with the towel, she thought about Craig. She was pleased that he understood that he couldn't just knock any time he wished, that he might be interrupting her. After all, she had her routines, and she didn't love the idea of people showing up unplanned.

Back in her room, she selected simple attire – white sandals, faded jeans, and a sleeveless navy blue blouse. She'd noticed when picking up her food that the attire was casual. And she didn't want to dress up and give Craig the wrong impression, though she still hadn't decided what that might be. She pulled her damp hair into a loose bun at the base of her neck and finished securing it just as she heard a knock. She walked to the front hall and opened the door to Craig who looked exceedingly handsome as usual.

"You always look amazing," he said as he reached for her hand.

Nell was surprised at how natural it felt for his hand to securely hold hers. Sometimes things just fit. But, she reminded herself, he was still someone she was getting to know, and there was so much more to learn about this man such as whether he could be trusted with her secrets.

The drive to the café was less than ten minutes and, while the place was busy, they were shown to a nice corner table. They each ordered Greek salads and margaritas, with salt on the edge of the glasses.

"So, tell me about your day," he urged.

Nell placed her linen napkin across her lap then looked up at Craig. "Good happenings today. Some days are hard, losses and serious surgeries. Today it was positive. I gave fluids to three cats and two dogs, all had surgery yesterday. And I assisted Dr. Hill with other procedures, a couple of dental issues, a spay, that's about it. I love a day when no life is ended."

Craig looked at her, wanting to touch her hand, but – not wanting to push too hard – he reached for his water glass instead. "You really love the animals, don't you?"

"Yes, and you?"

Craig smiled. "It's why I joined NAPS. Not to say it's a perfect organization. Some of the people there are headstrong individuals who don't look at the whole picture. Most of the officers, though, are there to protect the animals because they care about them. But I know you've heard other outcomes."

Nell nodded as she took a sip of her drink. "Let's just say that there are officers who have been known to be unreasonable. But I'm sure there are others who are like you."

"Most of the people connected with NAPS have the best of intentions and make good decisions. I know that firsthand. I also know about the exceptions."

Their salads were served with warm rolls, and Nell was glad for the break in conversation.

"Tell me what you do with yourself on evenings like this. You have that great little house and your graves to tend, but what do you do for fun? I know you don't go out to play with the bears."

Nell laughed and looked at Craig as she took another sip of her drink. Placing it down on the table she said, "I keep busy. A house doesn't take care of itself, and I like to read. My evenings are usually pretty quiet, but I like it that way."

"What did you do when you lived in California?"

"I was kind of a homebody. Even if my parents went out to dinner with friends, they'd try to drag me along, but I liked the quiet of home."

"You must have dated."

Nell swallowed a bite of her salad. "A little, but I didn't enjoy it as much as some of my friends did. Getting to know someone is nerve-wracking, and if you get to know someone and you can't see yourself with them, it's awkward. Especially when you're in high school and have to keep seeing the person in the halls every day."

Craig nodded. "Yeah, I definitely witnessed some of that drama, even in college. So do you have thoughts on marriage, kids, a little cottage by a cemetery?"

Nell laughed. "Well, the cottage part I have, but that wasn't planned. I suppose I always figured I'd have a family of my own someday. But once I came here to Connecticut, I kind of focused on my work and on taking care of the cemetery, and filling my life with what I love."

Craig's look was pensive, as though he wanted to inquire if there was room in her life for him. "Tell me what you love."

Nell could feel her cheeks flush. "Other than the

aforementioned ways I fill my time, painting. There's a satisfaction in creating."

He was quiet for a few moments then asked, "Have you been to Bearstone Mountain Park?"

"No, I've heard of it, but I haven't gone there yet."

"How about a ride there when we finish our meal? The sun is still shining on the hills and the place is gorgeous."

Nell squirmed in her chair and reached for the last of her margarita. "Could we do that another time? I work again tomorrow, and I really have a few things I planned to take care of tonight."

Craig nodded but looked disheartened. "Of course, whatever works for you. I'm glad I was able to steal you away for a while."

They finished their meal in near silence, and when the check came, Craig paid. He wanted more time with her, but he knew that he didn't want to scare her away. She obviously had a life there long before he entered her world, and he needed to respect her boundaries. But he also knew that there was a connection between them that couldn't be explained and definitely deserved further exploration.

Nell stood, gathered her purse to her shoulder, then walked with Craig to his car. She didn't want their time together to end, yet her instinct was to keep him at arm's length. At least until she could figure him out.

Chapter Six

With night chores completed, the little ones nesting in their fresh hay, Nell slid off her sandals and lay across her bed. She propped her hands under her chin, elbows on the mattress's edge, and studied the field of stars set in a cobalt sky.

As a child in California, she had tried many times to count all that she could see. As a teenager, she decided to think of herself as a keeper of the stars, regularly locating the Big Dipper and Jupiter along with other constellations and constants. Now she smiled at the amazing little lights who always added hope to her day, forgiveness to unexpected storms.

She rolled over and sat up on the edge of her bed, unbuttoned her blouse, slipped out of her jeans, and donned a knee-length nightdress. The air from the screened windows was refreshing yet mildly damp. Rain was expected. She stood and left her clothing on a chair to be washed then sat down again to enjoy the stars. Tomorrow night they might disappear, hiding behind thick clouds. In the Berkshires she noticed that the stars were brighter than they'd appeared in California. She was grateful that there were no intrusive lights as there had been where she grew up.

She thought about Craig and wondered if he was asleep. His apartment over the bakery was adequate but certainly not a place she would want to inhabit. But she figured it was sufficient for a young man who was adventuresome enough to seek out local highlights, and it certainly offered more than a room at the inn. She thought about him asking her to go with him to Bearstone Mountain Park. She'd been told by Dr. Hill that it was a fabulous place to picnic, to wander well-kept paths, and to breathe enticingly healthy air. She would go there sometime soon – maybe with Craig.

She looked around her room in the semi-darkness and thought about how she wondered as a teen if she would always live in California. Her thoughts strayed to life in Ireland where she and her parents had gone for a two-week vacation. She loved it there, the simple homes and meadows, wild donkeys, and pets at every doorstep. It seemed right to her, and she was sad to leave for life back in America. Then Connecticut happened and suddenly she had everything she dreamed of – her cottage and the surrounding land gave her the feel of the meadows of Ireland, along with the Berkshire hills, the wildlife, the privacy, the clear night skies filled with sparkling jewels afar. Yes, she was still keeper of the stars.

Nell slipped her bare legs beneath a sheet and one light blanket, positioning herself so that she could rest on her side, the covers up over her shoulders, eyes to the sky. Within minutes she was asleep.

***

When morning came it brought sheets of rain, not uncommon in that part of her adopted state. Everything held the aroma of earth. The deep-rooted clusters of pines, the wild roses, and the birds – tweeting and singing as they bathed seemed thrilled. Nell sat on the edge of her bed and smiled at the wonder of it all.

She took each of the young squirrels a sliver of apple and then added their daily portions of sunflower seed and acorns. They had everything they needed to grow strong, and yet she still worried. The unknown was always on her mind even though she hadn't yet encountered any issues with her former little patients. They had all done well and were released to their natural haven behind her house. Nell tried to see notable markings on them before release and would then watch for them once they were free. Every morning she went from window to window in search of her little friends.

Dressed in her dark blue slacks and shirt for work Nell made herself a piece of toast, covered it in butter and raspberry jam, then made her way to the car and drove toward the clinic. She realized halfway there that she'd forgotten her lunch but decided she could adlib. There was no time to turn back.

"How are the kids?" Dr. Hill asked as Nell helped to

secure a small dog having blood drawn.

"They're doing great. I think they've all finished with the meds now. And they eat like crazy. Sharp little teeth take those acorns and make them disappear."

Dr. Hill smiled. "They're good at that. That's how they get teeth that take my gutters apart. My wife loves them just like you do. She's always buying something at the grocery store she thinks they'll like. Good thing you two don't have an affection for bears."

Nell laughed. "Well, if I saw a bear in trouble, I'd probably call *you*."

He glanced at her for a split second and said, "Gee, thanks."

At the end of the day Nell pulled into her driveway where she parked her car close to the front of the cottage. Taking the house key from her purse as she opened the car door, she slipped out of the seat and looked around at the rain-washed trees and blooms. Everything looked new. At the door she put the key into the catch and found it to be reluctant. She tried again and the door opened. Once inside she took a closer look at the lock and wondered what she'd done that was different. Nothing was visibly wrong and when she tried the key again it was fine. She locked the door, left her purse on the coat rack, and walked first to the squirrels. They sat up and looked at her, their bright little eyes observing their human mom. She whispered to them, checked their water, gave them more food, then closed their door and walked into her kitchen where she poured lemonade into a glass. While swallowing the icy-cold drink she spotted her apple, banana, and bottle of water she'd forgotten. Lunch at work had been a handful of grapes from the clinic's receptionist.

Changing into a pair of shorts and a jersey, Nell decided on a frozen meal for supper. Feeling starved from a very light lunch, she was going to enjoy dinner – a sweet potato roasted along with a rice medley. Within fifteen minutes the house was filled with an enticing fragrance and prospect for a hearty meal. She took her lemonade into the parlor where she sat down to look at her mail and wait for the oven bell to ring.

When the phone rang, it jarred her as she placed the mail on her lap off to a side table. The caller was Craig and she hesitated before answering.

"Hi. I just wanted you to know," he said, "I went past your place early this morning and I stopped because your car was gone but your front door was open."

"What? I don't understand. What do you mean by open?"

"It was wide open. I went past, slowed the car, and backed up into your driveway. I had no idea what had caused you to go off with the door open. Trying to lure in a bear?" he teased.

While Nell didn't think that question was funny, she felt stunned and tried to recall what was going on that she would have done such a thing. She'd been in a hurry, she'd forgotten her lunch. She was now horrified to think of the risk she'd caused. Not only could someone have gone in and helped themselves to her belongings, but the squirrels. Someone could have seen the squirrels.

"What did you do?" she asked in almost a panic. "Did you see anything strange? I must have been distracted. Wow, I need to be careful."

"Yes, I would say that you do need to be careful. I doubt there are too many burglars in these parts, but quite honestly, anything could have wandered into your house. Are you okay? Does everything seem in place?"

Nell stood and began to walk around. Nothing seemed touched or removed. "Everything seems fine."

"Good. I drove past the clinic to see if your car was there after I closed your door, and of course it was. I kind of figured you'd taken off in a hurry for work and hadn't secured the cottage."

Nell took a deep breath as the oven bell rang. She wasn't as hungry now, but she gave her thanks to Craig, hung up the phone, then went to take the food out of the oven.

For a long while she sat and stared at the steaming food, annoyed with herself for leaving the door open.

After all her concern for anyone discovering the squirrels, she put them in danger with carelessness. That would not happen again. Once the rice dish seemed to have cooled enough to consume, she poked at it and the sweet potato, eating less than half. She kept reliving the morning and her rush to get to work, and she kept scolding herself for being a threat to her small patients.

At close to eight she realized she owed Craig a better thank you than her voice revealing hysteria. She dialed his number and in less than a moment he picked up.

"Are you okay?" he asked.

"Yes, I'm fine, and I just wanted to thank you again for saving me by closing my front door. I can't believe I did that, but I was in a hurry. I can't let that happen again. Really, Craig, you're a life saver."

She could envision him smiling as he asked, "Are you sure there isn't a bear sleeping in your bed? You know, the Goldilocks break-in?"

Nell laughed. "I checked everywhere, even *under* the bed. It's a shock to your system when you do something so stupid. I don't know how to thank you."

"I could suggest a nice way to thank me," he said. "But don't take this wrong, you don't have to do anything you don't want to do."

Nell smiled to herself, glad that he couldn't see her. "Like what?"

"I was hoping we could go to Bearstone Mountain Park. Maybe this weekend? We could pack a picnic and spend a couple of hours poking around. From what I've been told, we'll both love it there."

Nell drew in her breath, considering her options. Finding him alluring was not in her favor, she needed to keep him away from her squirrels. But, then again, the park was definitely *away* from her cottage.

The silence was prolonged, so he asked if she was still there. When she finally responded, he could hear in her voice that she was reluctant. "Are we okay?"

Nell felt guilty for being so evidently cautious with him. "Sorry, yes, we're okay. I'm just figuring out what I need to do over the next few days. I'll probably need to mow the cemetery over the weekend, but maybe we could take a couple of hours for the mountain. I've been wanting to go there."

She offered to pack a picnic and he offered to bring the drinks. It was settled, another date with Craig, a thank you of sorts for having closed her front door. In her heart she was excited; in her mind she was annoyed with herself for having been careless and for having given into his plea for her to join him at the park. She would prepare their picnic, potato salad, fresh tomato sandwiches and chocolate cake. That menu on her mind, Nell sat down to properly scold herself before going to bed.

With Saturday morning appearing in bright sun and

a light breeze, Nell dressed in shorts and a jersey, took care of the squirrels, and then poured herself a cup of coffee. She walked outside, this time being sure to close the door. She walked to the cemetery where the grass was plush from rain but would be fine for another day. Craig would be there to pick her up at eleven, so she had two hours to tend to a few tasks and to prepare the picnic.

The stream of excitement within her was noticeable. She wondered if it was a fair mix of being enthused about spending time with Craig or of being agitated by the complications this relationship posed. Either way, she was going to try her best to enjoy the day in a place she'd not yet visited with someone she was realistically, almost fervently, drawn to. Yet the relationship was riddled with impossibility.

The next hour was spent filling bird and squirrel feeders, sweeping out the shed, and then pulling a few weeds. A warm breeze gently stirred her surroundings and she decided that it was a good time to head back to the cottage to prepare the food.

After enjoying a glass of cold lemonade, she packed a tablecloth and napkins, then put the sandwiches together and took two small plastic containers of potato salad from the fridge. She added a couple of forks and cake to the basket then grabbed a blanket from her linen closet and draped it over the basket's handle before going to change into a pair of jeans and a

69

fresh shirt. She brushed her hair, applied a light skim of lipstick to her lips, and called that good enough.

Promptly at eleven, Craig was at her door. He looked at her from head to toe and smiled. "What? No hiking boots?"

Reaching for the picnic basket he used his other hand to reach for hers. She placed her hand in his without thinking of the intimacy. It came naturally.

"I don't see *you* wearing hiking boots," she said as she closed and locked her front door.

Craig laughed. "That's because I don't own any. That's okay though. I'm thinking we'll hike trails today that are appropriate for sneakers. No huge rock formations to scale, no broken limbs to scamper over like a squirrel. We'll be fine on the well-padded paths."

Nell felt a surge of fright as he mentioned squirrels, but then she relaxed. There was an abundance of them in this area, and it was a simple comment to make.

Craig opened her car door and she slipped inside. He set the basket and blanket on the floor in back of her then seated himself behind the steering wheel.

"No mowing today?" he asked as she gazed out her side window at passing fields bursting with corn.

She glanced over at him as she replied. "No, I'll get to that tomorrow."

"I could help you with that. If you make me breakfast, I'll be at your house by eight and get that

70

cemetery in good shape. What do you think?"

"Thank you, but I like to do the mowing myself. It gives me a chance to check on each grave and to fuss with the flowers, pulling weeds, taking note of moss against the stones. But thank you, I do appreciate the offer of help."

Craig looked over at her for a moment as he drove and wondered what to make of her on and off again demeanor. He decided to give the plan one more try with a hint of humor. "So, no breakfast?"

Nell flinched and hoped it didn't show. "Sorry, no breakfast. While all of our time together has been enjoyable, it's not the pace of life I'm used to. Sometimes I just need time to be alone, to take care of my responsibilities."

He nodded understanding as they pulled into the parking lot for Bearstone. Both were quiet as he removed their picnic items from the car and walked to the gate where they paid an entry fee and their hands were adorned with a bumblebee stamp by a park ranger. He nodded at the handsome young couple and advised them on the best route to take since rain earlier in the week had caused a few ruts on the main path.

After an hour of walking the elevated area until they were about a quarter of the way up the mountain, Craig chose a large flat rock and suggested they could take a break and enjoy lunch. He lifted bottles of ice cold water from his backpack as Nell opened the basket revealing a tempting assortment of food as well as a pretty flowered cloth and napkins. They had no need for the blanket.

"This," Craig said as he loosened the cap on her water, "is my idea of a really perfect day. The weather couldn't be better, the picnic looks delicious, and I couldn't have dreamed up better company."

Nell could feel her cheeks flush as she looked down, unpacking the sandwiches and potato salad. She passed a fork, tub of potato salad, and a sandwich to Craig, then a napkin. "It is beautiful here," she said. "I can smell the cedar. Everything is so nice when it's been recently washed by Mother Nature. There really isn't anything you could buy that would compare to what's right here. Thank you for suggesting it. This is wonderful."

"There's something I discovered when I checked into this place on my computer last night. They have an enthusiastic group who meet here several nights a year. They call themselves The Gazers because they have telescopes to view the stars. It must be outstanding from up here, a sky scattered with diamonds. The peace and quiet alone must be remarkable. Maybe we could tag along with them some time."

Nell thought about the evening before, sitting on the edge of her bed, her eyes fastened to the specks of light in the dark summer sky. "I'm sure it's incredible up here. There's not a shred of light from anywhere to intrude or compete with the stars. I was always into the constellations as a kid, picking out the Big Dipper and Orion's Belt. I especially loved when I could find Ursa Minor. And here we are, on Bearstone Mountain."

Craig looked at her beautiful face as he unwrapped his sandwich and took a bite. "Well then, it's a date," he said as he cleaned mayonnaise from his lips.

Once again, Nell reprimanded herself silently for having created a mood regarding star-gazing. Now how was she going to get out of this?

After lunch they sat on the rock with their water and watched as birds, chipmunks, and squirrels gratefully accepted crumbs from their sandwiches. "I bet there are bears up here just waiting to see what we've left behind of our food," Craig said.

Nell looked around and thought he was quite possibly right. "I'm sure the rangers would discourage our generosity. We wouldn't want the bears to become accustomed to human offerings as they could become a risk and need to be removed."

Craig looked at her and smiled. "See? You're adapting to the NAPS philosophy, keeping the animals safe by not introducing them to human ways."

Nell looked him in the eyes without returning a smile. "I would never endanger a wild animal with my own selfish thought of seeing it up close. But there are times when helping them is a necessity to supporting their lives. I believe in helping them. Sometimes that's with an offering of food in a treacherous winter. It's bad enough they have to brave the zero temperatures and heavy snow. Finding food is often a challenge."

"True. That's why I think it's wonderful that you have bird and squirrel feeding stations around your property. I bet all sorts of creatures have enjoyed the seed – raccoons, skunks, chipmunks. Do you put any other food out?"

Nell was hesitant to reply but wasn't going to lie. "I have, but not at my house. I've left bags of dry dog food and sometimes bread with peanut butter a few acres from me or anyone else. Always on my property, but not close enough for them to associate the food with my place. I doubt that's promoted by NAPS though."

"While you're right, NAPS would probably go with the advice to let nature take its course, it sounds like you're not doing anything to cause a problem."

"That's why I stay clear of NAPS," she said. "They take every case as being invasive and damaging, and it's not."

"I think you're right about that," Craig said as he stood. "Shall we pack up our lunch and climb a little further?"

Without answering, Nell stood and gathered what was left back into the basket. Craig picked it up and took the blanket from her, placed his backpack over

74

one shoulder, and he reached again for her hand. Protective as he was, Nell felt cherished and wished she didn't.

They climbed for another hour before stopping to drink more water. The ledge where they stood had a view that would be perfect for star watching. Neither of them said a word about that as each of them scanned the cloudless sky in silence.

Going down the mountain didn't take as long. The ground wasn't too steep, and they were able to pass the time commenting on little creatures they saw. Craig pointed out a small harmless snake sunning itself nearby and identified some botanical interests.

Back at his car with their belongings packed in the back seat, Craig opened the passenger door for Nell then walked to the driver's side and slid behind the wheel. He started the engine and glanced at his pleasing guest.

"I'm glad you were able to come with me today," he said as they pulled out of the parking lot and onto the main road. "Would you like to watch the stars some night up there? I'm thinking it would be quite a show."

"I'm sure it's beautiful, but I guess we'll need to see about our timing."

Craig wasn't sure what she meant. "You mean how busy you are when I suggest an evening?"

"Yes, I mean, you can certainly go without me. You might meet more people like yourself, star enthusiasts."

Craig felt confused but stayed silent. It was as though Nell was pushing him away, hoping he might meet someone else more to his liking. He doubted that could ever happen, but something was keeping Nell bound to her duties and to a semi-isolated existence.

They drove the fifteen minutes to her house in silence. He did not push to see her that night. He lifted her basket and blanket from his car then walked her to the door. He thanked her for accompanying him to the park then turned and left.

Nell stood inside her cottage with the basket and blanket in her hands. She looked down at them and tears fell as she placed the two items on a chair. She walked to the bathroom where she ran cold water over her hands and then splashed more onto her face. She liked him too much.

Chapter Seven

For days after their hike at Bearstone Mountain, Nell was busy working an extra two days at the clinic to make up for another tech on vacation. The entire time, she thought about Craig and wondered why he hadn't stopped by or called. She wanted to be with him yet knew she could not, and now she was fearful that she had pushed him too far away. She understood that she seemed inconsistent in her reactions to him, and she knew she could be difficult to get along with when it came to the subject of animals. They were inconveniently on opposite sides, and there was no negotiation recognizable in this situation.

Two full weeks went by without Nell seeing or hearing from Craig. She went into town, careful not to cross his path at the bakery, yet never saw his car parked to the side of the building. She wondered if he'd moved, and that thought left her feeling empty, exceptionally sad. Even though there was no good way to have Craig in her life, that didn't stop her from missing him. Unreasonably, she wished he'd never stopped at her cottage to visit his grandfather's grave.

After eighteen days in a row of seeing nothing of

Craig, Nell walked to the cemetery to water the blooms at the graves. Some of them were looking wilted, some she would replace. As she stood from crouching down to remove a few weeds from one grave, she turned and found herself face to face with him just inches away.

"I see duty calls," he said. "You keep this place like a personal garden, Nell. It's really beautiful."

She stepped back a foot or two and looked at his handsome face. "Thank you. It's important to me."

Craig looked around at the meadows and hills beyond the cemetery. The area was entrancing as was the grave tender. "I thought about calling you a few times while I was away but decided not to disturb you. How've you been?"

Nell looked away from him then back at his penetrating eyes. "Fine, busy. I picked up a few extra days at the clinic – another tech was on vacation."

Craig nodded. "I see. Well, I had to make an unplanned trip to California. My parents were in an accident and hospitalized."

"Are they okay?" Nell asked as she brushed dirt from her hands.

"They are now, but it could have been bad. Dad had his foot broken, so he's home hobbling around on crutches. Mom broke a couple of ribs. The two of them are hurting some, but I got them situated with groceries, frozen meals to make things easier, and, well, they're fine."

"That's the scary part about living a distance away," Nell said.

"Yes, it definitely is. But there are family members who help one another out there. They'll be okay, and I'll keep an eye on them long distance."

"Would you move back to California?"

Craig looked at her and half smiled. "I can't imagine doing that. Would you?"

Nell looked around at the sun-drenched area and felt a light breeze across her arms and face. "I could never leave here."

She started to move away from him and he turned to follow. They were silent until they reached Nell's side yard close to where Craig had left his car. They stopped and she turned to face him. "Well, welcome back. It's nice to see you again. I'm glad your family is mending well." She began to walk toward her door when he stopped her by reaching for her right hand.

"Nell, I thought about calling you every day I was there. But, honestly, the last time we were together, I had these dark thoughts that maybe you wanted me to leave you alone. By the time I was on my way back, I was worried about how you'd greet me. I'm a little confused, uncertain, something along those lines. The truth is, when I'm with you I feel complete. When I'm away from you, even just down the street over the bakery, I feel empty. Am I reading you right? Do you want me to stay clear of here? I mean I can visit my grandfather's grave without bothering you if that's what you want."

Nell slipped her hand out of his gently and brushed her hair back from her face. She looked down at the ground then up at her front door before looking at Craig.

"Should I just go?" he asked.

Nell swallowed back emotion, begging her body not to betray her with tears. "It's just weird – the way we met, the things we have in common, and the things we differ about. I'm not sure we're a good fit."

The silence was deep. Nell looked at the cluster of pines not far from her cottage as Craig stared at her eyes. After several long minutes Craig finally said, "Okay then, I'll be going."

Inside the cottage, cool with afternoon shade, Nell sat down in her favorite parlor chair and leaned forward until her long hair fell over her knees. The tears flowed and her heart felt damaged. Craig was so right for her, and so wrong for her. She sat up straight, walked to the bathroom and splashed cool water on her tear-stained face, then walked to the back room where she checked on the squirrels. They were each curled into a ball, their long tails wrapped around them, sleeping. There was absolutely no doubt in her mind, taking care of little animals was first. Finding a life partner would have to be an absolute positive. It would need to be with someone who understood that it wasn't right in any way to kill an ill or wounded creature if it could be helped.

With a heavy sense of loss, Nell spent the next week working two extra days again, filling in for vacationing techs.

"I don't know how I'd manage without you, Nell," Dr. Hill said as she assisted him in drawing blood from a German Shepherd.

"I'm always willing to help," she said as she stroked the dog's neck. "You help me with the medicine and advice for my little ones too. I'm grateful to you for that."

"Are they getting big?"

Nell smiled. "They are. I can't believe how well they're doing. One of them is really ready to go, but I want to release all three together, maybe in another couple of weeks. I know they'll love being outside, and my shed has windows that open so they can be inside if they choose. I'll miss them though."

Dr. Hill looked at her and nodded. "You've been through this before. I remember you coming in here last year in tears because you'd released two others, the red ones I think."

Nell smiled. "Yes, the red ones, Jimmy and Billy. I still see them often. They bicker sometimes over acorns and the seed I put out for the birds, but basically, they play, scampering up and down the tree just outside my kitchen window."

***

At home that night Nell first checked on the squirrels. They had food and water and were fine. She poured herself a cold drink and sat down to ponder what she wanted for dinner – maybe a grilled cheese sandwich, maybe a crisp salad. She thought about her evening with Craig when they'd had dinner together, and the picnic at Bearstone Mountain. He had been wonderful company.

As much as she missed him, Nell knew in her heart that this was for the best, that taking care of wildlife was always going to be an important factor in her life. She was confident that how she was treating them, with a bit of assistance from Dr. Hill, was the right thing. NAPS could go rescue the animals in the hands of inexperienced others, but they needed to leave her alone. She would do anything to protect her passion, the innocents of the land.

***

Two weeks passed and it became evident that her three patients were no longer in need of her assistance. They were strong and playful, ready to go before summer's end and cooler nights found them nesting in trees. With tears and promises to them, she carried their cages to the shed so they could become familiar with it. After another three days, she opened their cages, removed the window screen, and they were free. For several nights after, all three returned to their little beds, and then one night they were gone. She looked for them the next morning and spotted them running after one another on the ground below her kitchen window tree. She smiled through tears – there they were, healthy and independent, just as she'd planned.

The empty room was thoroughly cleaned out in case another needed the space to heal and grow. When she closed the door leading from there to her kitchen, she felt a deep sense of loss. *I'll never be able to endure having kids and see them go off to college. I might as well plan to live here like a hermit forever.*

Grocery shopping in town a few days later, she thought about going to the bakery for a loaf of rye when she spotted Craig at his car. She turned back into the store, pretended to have forgotten a package of cheese, paid for it, and then left. By that time, Craig was gone and she immediately wondered where. Was he off on a date with some normal girl who had a life not quite so underhanded?

Driving home she felt weighted with feelings she had failed to expel. She knew that Craig was not someone she'd ever forget. He was everything she thought she'd never know.

There were times when she wondered if she'd have preferred never meeting him. He'd been electrifying from the first moment, like nothing she'd ever felt before. She decided that it was plain foolish to go with the old saying, *better to love and lose then never love at all*. Their relationship was impossible, but now that she knew he existed, she felt the loss of him, and it hurt.

Each night as she gazed at the stars in the distant sky, she questioned why Craig and she had been thrust together. Was there significance in their grandfathers being friends, of the California connection, their last names being identical, a shared love for watching those faraway glimmers of light? Why did they ever have to meet? It was obviously all their grandfathers' fault.

***

Just a few steps from her car one morning, Nell looked up in time to see Craig driving past. She started to wave to him but there was no sign that he'd seen her and within moments he was around the bend, out of sight. Again that lingering sadness swept through her as she slipped behind the wheel and started her engine. No squirrels to take care of, no Craig to come for pancakes. She had her regrets, but a man like him wasn't going to stay available for long. She thought he must certainly be dating and had more than likely put her in his rearview mirror – literally and figuratively.

***

September brought color to the sugar maples surrounding the area, and Nell noted that the grave blooms needed to be changed. Day after day she bought chrysanthemums in a variety of colors and planted them until all seventy-four graves looked ready for cooler temperatures and autumn's glowing display. This was her favorite time of year in the Berkshires. The foliage was brilliant in varying shades of orange, gold, and red, and the animals scurried about storing nature's gift of food and nesting materials. Then Thanksgiving and Christmas, Nell's favorites would follow.

She wondered if Craig would return to California to have Thanksgiving with relatives. She would be spending extra hours at the clinic, allowing a few who had families nearby to enjoy more time off for shopping and gathering. She would have pumpkins at her doorstep, a tree for Christmas, but she would remain there at the cottage when not at the clinic. And despite her best efforts, she would think about Craig.

Chapter Eight

In early October Nell found herself feeling very much alone and knew that it was about Craig more than anything else. She'd lived perfectly fine for two years without dating, without feeling solitary. Every Sunday she called her parents, most Wednesdays they called her. Friends from California disappeared, getting married, having babies, moving away. Nell kept up with two of them for the first year after moving to Connecticut. She'd been a maid of honor for one and a bridesmaid for the other. They'd been close, but Nell found that things change once a marriage partner enters the scene. She was the odd one out.

In the clinic's surgery room early one morning after Dr. Hill finished a spaying and then two neuters, Nell was asked to do him a favor. She would refuse him nothing as he'd been like another father.

"What do you need?"

Dr. Hill looked at her over his spectacles while washing his hands. "I have a wild rabbit we found in our yard. It's not young. It's a female, probably about a year old. She had a tear on her right rear leg -- probably from a branch, maybe a fence. I gave her a little gas to calm her, treated the wound and stitched her up, but she needs to stay in a safe place until it's healed. Could you take her for a week or two? When she's ready to be released, I'll take her back to my yard where she knows her way around. I never know when I'll be inspected and having a wild rabbit wouldn't go over well."

"Of course I'll take her. I haven't had a wild rabbit yet. Does she need medicine?"

"Nope, she's good. She just needs to be safe and quiet. I wrapped her leg securely. Before she goes off on her way, I'll gas her lightly again and take a good look. She's going to be fine with a little rest."

***

Nell took the caged brown rabbit home and transferred her to one of the large squirrel cages after lining it with fresh hay and a soft blanket. Nell added a water bottle and a dish containing a mix of sunflower seed and bits of kale and cucumber then decided to pick up pellets the next day. She watched her for a few minutes as the nervous little creature licked at her bandaged leg and then gave up and washed her front paws and face. Nell turned the light off and left her to rest, the finishing touch after having a surgical procedure.

At the grain store the next day, her day off, Nell bought two pounds of rabbit pellets and a good-sized pumpkin for her front step. As she placed the beautiful autumn piece down, turning it so that the stem was visible from the road, she looked up to see Craig pulling into her driveway. She stood upright and watched as he left his car and walked toward her.

"That's a pretty nice pumpkin," he said. "How have you been?"

Nell wondered if she could speak without crying. "Okay. How are you?"

"I'm fine, thanks. I've had a lot of work added to my job, so I've been living a lot like a monk. How are things at the clinic?"

"Busy. Everyone around here prefers Dr. Hill over the big hospitals. He's wonderful, very caring and not expensive."

"What's in the bag?" Craig asked as he pointed to the rabbit pellets.

Nell thought fast. "It's rabbit pellets. I picked them up at the grain store for Dr. Hill." That was no lie and Craig nodded without further question.

"I actually have something for you," he said. "Hold on for a minute – I'll get it." He walked to the car's back door and returned to Nell with a small bag. "I saw this when I was in California and thought of you. It seemed to call your name."

Nell opened the bag and lifted a tissue wrapped item into her hands, opening it carefully. She swallowed hard when she saw a glass star, cobalt blue with specks of what looked like metal fragments embedded in its

88

three-inch surface. She held it, unable to take her eyes from the beautiful piece.

"I don't know what to say," she half whispered. "It's just so perfectly beautiful, Craig."

"I'm glad you like it. It's been riding around with me for a while now."

"Thank you so much," she said and wiped away the tears from her face.

They stared at one another for what seemed a long time before she asked if he'd like a cup of reheated coffee from the morning. Having a rabbit would not present a problem – they were quiet creatures and she felt sure it would fine.

"I'd love one," he said.

Inside he sat down at the center island as though he did it every day. He watched as she heated the brew and placed mugs and napkins on the island, no milk or sugar for either of them.

"I've always loved this room," he said. "It's spacious for a cottage, and it's friendly."

Nell laughed. "I've never heard a room described as friendly."

"But it is. Don't you feel it? Look at this place. Everything here is useful yet pretty. Did you decorate or was it this way when you came?"

"Half and half. My grandfather was a very neat man. The place was welcoming and efficient. I added the mugs, the curtains, and the red glass sphere in the window over the sink."

Nell poured the steaming coffee into their mugs and then sat down. "I have nothing good to go with this. I should make some cookies or something."

"Yes," he said with a serious tone, "you should," and then he smiled.

Nell wanted to reach out for his beautiful hands but instead she took a sip from her coffee.

They were quiet for a few moments before Craig asked if Nell was seeing anyone.

"You mean romantically?"

Craig looked at her for a moment then laughed. "Yes, I guess that's what I mean."

Nell smiled. "No, I've been pretty busy. I grocery shop and go to work. Otherwise I'm here tending to the cemetery and keeping my cottage in order."

Craig nodded. "I love this place. It felt like home the very first time you invited me in when we met."

Nell understood exactly what he meant. The first day she arrived from California, weary from the flight and then having rented a car until she could buy one of her own, she walked into the cottage in awe.

"Are you going to your family for the holidays?" he asked seemingly out of the blue.

"No," Nell said shaking her head. "I'm working a lot around Thanksgiving and Christmas, filling in for married people. And my mom and dad won't be home anyway. They're taking a Christmas cruise to Catalina with my aunt and uncle. They invited me along, but, no, I'm staying right here."

Craig swallowed some coffee then placed his mug down on the marble surface. "I'm staying here, too. My family is gathering in San Diego for Thanksgiving and Big Bear for Christmas. It's nice in both places, but I'm staying here. I've been looking around for a larger apartment, maybe a small house. Above the bakery is great, but I'd eventually like something with a yard."

Nell nodded and asked if he'd like more coffee. "I don't have anything wonderful to eat in the house, but I could offer you toast and jam, or..."

"No, thank you for the offer of sustenance but the coffee is good. Maybe we could go grab a bite someplace later, unless you're busy."

Nell looked at Craig then at her coffee.

"Nell, I'm not sure where to go with our whatever-it-is. Can we at least be friends? Can we be that to one another? For the weeks when we didn't see each other, I missed you. I thought we had a lot in common, and look at where we live, in a little New England town where we're bound to bump into one another. I'd love it if we could stay connected, you know, friends, star-gazers."

Nell looked up at him. He was direct in his feelings, charming in his approach to honesty. She wanted him in her life, but she didn't know if she could just be friends with him. And even in friendship, his dropping by, would be complicated.

"If we could take things slow," she began, "see one another when the timing is good for each of us, I think being friends would be nice." Nell picked up the glass star he'd given her. "Star-gazing would be fun some night."

Craig nodded and smiled. "Yes, it certainly would. And this evening, are you free? We could grab a bite to eat someplace and then try for Bearstone's sky watch. Maybe?"

His smile was so winning that she laughed. "You don't give up easily, do you?"

He looked at her and said, "I don't give up when something feels right to me."

***

That October evening, with a distinct chill in the mountain air, Craig stopped his car in her driveway and walked to the cottage. He was about to knock when Nell opened the door wearing jeans and a cherry red sweater. She pulled a jacket from the coat rack, tucked her ID into her pocket, smiled at her companion, then walked with him to his car.

"I thought we might try Spring Brook Café again. Those margaritas we had were pretty good as I recall."

Nell smiled. "If I'm going to search for the constellations, I think I'll keep my mind sharp with hot cider."

Craig slipped behind the wheel as she fastened her seatbelt. "Not a bad idea. Hot cider would be good."

Just after seven they drank the last of their cider having finished homemade mac and cheese with wide-cut noodles, Nell's choice, which Craig followed.

At the parking lot for Bearstone Mountain they found a sandwich board for the star gazing group, providing directions for which path to take and where to get a flashlight if one hadn't been brought. Craig had two in his car, so they were set for the hike up toward Cliffton Notch. Craig smiled and informed her that he knew the place as he'd gone hiking a couple of times while they were apart.

As they climbed a mellow then steep incline, Craig reached for Nell's hand and pulled her gently along on their adventure. Nell loved the warmth of his hand over hers, the consideration he extended as they moved carefully above the town. At one point Nell turned to look down and could barely see faint lights from the occasional car and from the police station. It was so quiet, so peaceful. She thought about how much she loved being with Craig.

After twenty minutes, both of them slightly out of breath and laughing at themselves, they met a group of about twenty people, all ages. People turned as they joined in and welcomed them as they introduced themselves.

"You're gonna love this show," an older gentleman

said. "Here, take a look through my telescope. You'll be able to see the map of the gods."

Craig took the three-foot telescope from the man after thanking him, then after a quick look, passed it to Nell. When she almost fell backward, he stood behind her with his hands on her shoulders while she pointed it to the sky filled with wonder.

"Oh, there's the Big Dipper and Little Dipper. Oh, this is incredible," she said.

After a few moments she handed the telescope back to Craig. He looked again and pointed to other constellations and stars that seemed like they were dancing. After a few minutes, they returned the telescope to the man who had introduced himself as Gus, thanking him for the close-up he'd provided. The group was welcoming, every one of them enthusiastic about the magical brilliance so far away.

The chill of night air on the mountain became too much for some, and one by one they left, leaving just nine viewers, including Nell and Craig.

"Are you getting cold?" he asked her.

Nell smiled and shivered. "Just a little."

He wrapped his arm around her shoulders and pulled her close to him. "Let's go. It's after ten. We've been here a long time. Maybe if we come again this time of year, we should wear heavier coats. It's my fault. I should have guessed it would be colder up here."

"Neither of us thought about that, but this is pure joy. I've loved every minute."

Craig was as close to her as he'd ever been. He was tempted to kiss her but held back.

They said goodnight to the remaining gazers and made their way down the mountain with the flashlights shining on the path just ahead of them. At the car, Craig held the door open while Nell settled in then went to his own side.

As she secured her seatbelt, Nell looked over at his profile in the dim light. "I loved this so much. Thank you, Craig, for the entire evening."

At the cottage, he walked her to the door. She felt certain that if she invited him in, he'd accept, but she didn't. It was close to eleven and there was work the next day. She would assist Dr. Hill in five different surgeries, all routine, but nevertheless, she wanted to be rested. No time for mistakes when it came to the animals.

"So we're going to be seeing each other," he said to clarify their relationship. "We're friends, right?"

Before she could reply he leaned in for a kiss and Nell found herself clinging to him for more. When they finally moved an inch apart, she looked into his eyes and they both smiled as they touched forehead to forehead, their hands entwined.

"I don't know about this friendship stuff," Nell said, and they laughed.

"I kind of like it," he said.

Nell smiled and turned to place her key in the latch. She took a step inside, turned to thank Craig again, then said goodnight. He stood for a moment after the door closed then turned and walked to his car.

Nell locked the door, took her jacket off, and walked to check on the rabbit. It was sleepy, aware of her presence, but not upset. She made sure the room was toasty, a healing animal needed warmth to mend properly. Closing the door against the kitchen light, she leaned against the island for a moment, touching where Craig had been hours before. This *friendship* of theirs was a bit more than she expected, yet it was sweet and very unforgettable. They'd made no definitive plans to see one another again, but she hoped. In the meanwhile, she needed to take a quick shower then get to bed.

As she pulled the covers over her legs and up to her chin, she looked out through her window to the endless sky and its tiny jewels. She knew that no matter how much her mind denied the possibility, her relationship with Craig was going to not only be memorable, but magnetic. By heartstrings she was fastened to him.

Chapter Nine

Six the next morning came with a darkened October sky. Nell made her bed, dressed in her clinic attire, then made her way to check on the rabbit. The food was gone, a good sign. Nell left a dish with pellets and a small handful of kale. This was hopeful, the bandage was still in place and the rabbit was not intimidated by being fostered while healing.

Nell walked to her kitchen, heated coffee, sipped it while making toast, ate, and then headed to work. The first surgery was at eight and four more would follow until sometime after noon. At that point she would have lunch, then draw blood and give fluids to whatever needed them. Nothing bothered her about taking care of animals – if they were to heal, they had to be treated, plain and simple.

That evening she changed out of her uniform and took a quick shower, climbed into a soft jersey lounge set, then set about her routine: rabbit, dinner, read.

Nell made herself a grilled cheese sandwich, her go-to-favorite, and deciding on tea, she had that in her parlor chair by a glowing hearth. It was all nearly perfect – adding one other ingredient would have made it so. Craig, she thought with a smile, would be a wonderful addition to this room, to this evening, to her.

She read more of her book and after ten decided she was tired enough for sleep. Sitting at the edge of her bed she looked toward the sky. The stars weren't showing quite as brilliant, clouds had served to cover them in a ghostly blanket filled with the promise of rain. Nell sighed and shifted her body beneath the covers, her eyes still to the sky.

She could not forget the ecstasy she'd enjoyed with Craig at her side on Bearstone Mountain, the constellations clear, the night air chilled. Beyond that sheer beauty was the company – the star-gazers they'd met, and of course holding Craig's hand. She thought how wonderful it must be to own that depth of emotion, to feel the delirium of being in love. But she had never really thought it would happen to her. Nell understood that she was different from other girls in her devotion to the sweet lives of the innocents. She didn't have faith that she could have it all, animals and a winsome man at her side. It was, she determined, going to break her in pieces when the time came to part with Craig, and while that was not her wish, it was, she felt, her destiny. But she decided to enjoy their relationship while it lasted.

The next day turned out to be hectic at the clinic. Two emergencies came in just minutes after the first surgery began. Nell was called to leave Dr. Hill's side as he completed a cat spaying to assist in tending to a dog that had been struck by a car. The trauma felt by the animal was as important as the injury. She and another technician began to prepare the examination table as Dr. Hill walked in, washed his hands thoroughly, then administered immediate calming and pain meds to the dazed dog. Within moments the heartbeat became close to normal. Dr. Hill left the dog's side to examine a cat that had collapsed at home, one emergency on top of the other. Once again, the cat was stabilized with a shot and began to breathe at an acceptable rate. Nell and another technician stood by, their hearts wildly beating at the prospect of losing either animal.

Within an hour the dog was examined, an x-ray had been done, and it was found to have a fractured right rear leg. Dr. Hill delivered quieting meds until he could go in and set the bone, casting it in place. The cat was found to have had a minor heart irregularity – the correct medication would take care of the problem, more than likely a life-long issue.

Everyone at the clinic scurried to make sure the emergency victims came first, their stabilization most important. By the end of the day, with one pet after another being seen, the doctor and his assistants were frazzled and exhausted. Nell had not had time or interest in lunch, but going home she thought about what she might fix for her dinner. She remembered the wonderful Greek salad she'd had with Craig, and considered calling something in to pick up, but she was tired, in need of a shower, and she'd settle for peanut butter on toast once she was in her pajamas.

Nell put two slices of bread in the toaster, then went to feed and check on the rabbit. She had just finished giving him his food when the toast popped up. After washing her hands, she spread the peanut butter on the warm bread, and enjoyed eating her meal along with a cup of tea.

Later, as she sat relaxed in her hearthside chair, the phone rang. She had an instant burst of hope that it was Craig. She picked up the phone and said, "Hello."

"Hello. Just checking in to see how you are, dear," her mother said.

Nell sat back in her chair and stared at the dark hearth wishing there was a fire there. "I'm fine. Busy day, but everything turned out well. How about you and Dad? Is everything good with you two?"

"Yes, we're both well, keeping busy. But I do have a question. Is there any chance we could lure you home for Thanksgiving? Your aunt and uncle are coming out from Philadelphia, and I was so hoping we could persuade you to join us."

"I can't, Mom. I offered to work extra hours at the clinic so married folks could have time with their families. One other tech and I will be holding down the fort, with Dr. Hill on call."

"Oh, I'm disappointed. I so hoped we'd see you over the holidays. You know we're going off to Catalina for Christmas, staying at that nice little inn you always loved. We miss having you around, honey. You're our significant burst of youth."

Nell laughed. "I'm not sure the term youth is relevant. I'm twenty-seven now you know."

"I do know," her mother replied with laughter. "I was there when you were born."

Nell laughed. "You were? Really?"

The two women laughed together.

"Well, if you're not coming home, I do hope you're going to have a wonderful dinner on Thanksgiving, hopefully with friends, and that Christmas will be your rendition of merry."

Nell smiled to herself. There were zero plans for Thanksgiving, which probably meant peanut butter toast again or grilled cheese, and Christmas likely the same. They chatted for a few more minutes before hanging up.

Her thoughts now on the holidays, Nell wondered what Craig had planned – he'd already said he was staying in Connecticut. Maybe, just maybe, they'd find some celebratory time together.

While Nell was off from the clinic the next three days she decorated the iron-gate entrance to the cemetery with straw bales and pumpkins, lavender and yellow chrysanthemums off to each side. She vacuumed her house, took care of her recuperating little guest, then decided to make two pumpkin pies – one for Benjamin, the elderly gentleman who kept the clinic sparkling clean, and the other for herself. After all, what was fall without delicious pies and breads?

Having baked and finished her tidying, Nell decided to drive into town to pick up more kale for the bunny and maybe a loaf of bread for herself. In her heart, she hoped she would see Craig, but she knew he was working long hours and that he might not be aware just how close she was. She smiled – she hoped.

The trip into town was quick and simple, no sign of Craig except for his car which was parked next to the bakery. After placing her groceries behind her seat, Nell looked over at the windows of his apartment then climbed into her car and drove home.

She unpacked and put away the few items she bought, then with dusk near, she decided to light a fire in the hearth and sort through her paints. Some of them were old, remnants of California, and she decided to let them go. When she'd sorted the blues in to one space, the burnt umber and gold tones into another, she felt ready to paint, maybe the next day in northern light.

She watched the fire dance then found herself thinking about the stars in her world. Sitting back in her chair, Nell felt soothed by the notion that she had so very much to be grateful for.

Poking at the fire with a piece of kindling she

settled back into her chair and pulled an afghan over her legs. It had been a gift from her grandmother, her father's mother, who had often said two things about Nell – her hair was her crown and glory and that she was an old soul.

The old soul part was probably true. So much of who Nell was differed from others her age. Never impressed by fancy dresses and sprightly parties, Nell considered the fact that maybe she was just unsociable, no fun, or maybe a legitimate introvert.

Her thoughts were interrupted by the sound of the gravel on her driveway crunching as a car pulled in. She stood and looked out through the parlor window and smiled as she saw Craig walking up the steps. She opened the door to a raised fist ready to knock.

"Well this is the kind of service I like," he said. "I was driving past and decided to chance stopping to say hello. So, hello."

Nell smiled and invited him in. "Nice to see you," she said closing the door.

"I was thinking I'd pick up a sub someplace since I worked through lunch today. But then I had a better idea. Any interest in going for a bite?"

Nell gestured toward the hearth. "I'm afraid I'm in for the night. I love a wood fire, but it's not something one can easily just turn off."

Craig nodded and walked further into the room. "What smells so good in here?"

"Could be pumpkin pie I made earlier."

"One of my favorites," he said with a wink.

"Mine too," she admitted. "I haven't eaten yet either. If you'd like, you can join me for some soup and one of my famous grilled cheese sandwiches, then pumpkin pie."

"I accept that invitation, and with the fire going, this is pretty perfect."

"Take your jacket off, sit down. I won't be long in the kitchen."

"Oh, no," he said as he left his jacket across a chair, "I'm going to watch this miracle you perform making a grilled cheese. The ones I make are always too soggy."

Nell smiled as they walked to the kitchen where Craig sat down at the island. "You probably use too much butter or margarine and at too low a heat level. You need that medium heat and to not allow the bread to swim in moisture. Olive oil works well too. It's easy."

"For you, yes. But I'll observe; I'm a fair learner. Got any coffee in that pot?"

Nell turned, passed him a mug, then instructed him to heat some in the microwave from the French press. "One minute," she said. "That will make it the right temperature for sipping."

Craig stood and smiled. "See, I'm taking note and learning all this good stuff. I guess I should have paid more attention to my mom's cooking. I ate it…that's about it."

Nell prepared the sandwiches and heated tomato soup from a can. She turned to him as he sat back down. "You still have time to learn."

"But if I keep you around, I won't have to."

Nell half smiled at him but felt a chill at the same time. She could picture herself around Craig all the time, and then she halted her romantic emotions and remembered she had a wild rabbit in a room just six feet away from where he sat.

"Okay," she said with the browned sandwiches on plates, the soup in bowls, "let's take this in by the fire. I have a nice little table by the sofa, and we'll have the luxury of ambience."

Craig helped by taking the tray of food into the parlor while Nell fetched glasses of water, spoons, and napkins. The room conspired to create the perfect setting, a glowing hearth and good company.

Craig spread a napkin across his lap and took a bite of the sandwich, closed his eyes for a moment, then commented, "This is ideal. A real story-book setting. You're something special, Nell McGann. Thank you for inviting me."

"You've taken me to dine with you a few times, so this is the very least I could do. I'm sorry not to have something more dinner-like. I can cook, I promise."

"Oh, good. So, what's for Thanksgiving? It's not too far away you know."

"Yes," Nell nodded, "I'm aware. If you'd care to join me, maybe I'll do something a little more impressive than grilled cheese."

He laughed. "Excellent. Maybe I can help with the prep. What will we make?"

Nell sat back in her chair. "How about stuffed squash, real mashed potatoes, cranberry sauce, and green bean casserole?"

"Sounds fantastic. Mind if I also bring along some corn on the cob? I hear it's what the pilgrims ate."

Nell stood and laughed as she turned to collect their dishes and head to the kitchen. "I think that sounds doable. Would you like me to cut you a piece of pumpkin pie?"

"Yes, please."

"Whipped cream or no?"

"I'll have what you're having."

Nell returned with two slices of pie, each adorned with a little squirt of whipped cream, and two cups of black coffee.

Craig took a mouthful and dabbed at his lips with a napkin. "This is the best pumpkin pie I've ever had."

"You can thank my mother and my grandmother. I learned about cooking and baking from them."

"Will I get to do that someday?"

"Do what, cook and bake?"

"I was thinking the part about thanking your mother and grandmother."

Nell could feel her face flush. "Well, my mom maybe, but unfortunately my grandmother is gone."

"I'm sorry."

Nell nodded. "Me too."

After a few moments of silence Craig said, "So it's a plan? We'll do Thanksgiving together, right here in this great house with the fire going?"

Nell nodded. "Yes, we'll do this."

The evening ended after nine when Craig noticed Nell's sleepy eyes. "I'm going to head out. You look tired and I actually need to get up at four in the morning for a conference call to England, nine their time. Maybe we could grab a coffee someplace tomorrow afternoon, or whenever you're available."

Nell stood and walked with him to the door. They hesitated, each not making a move toward the other. "Let's see what the day brings."

"Thank you for a delicious meal and the wonderful company," he said.

As he began to lean toward her, Nell accepted his light kiss to her cheek. A full kiss on the lips would have been more to her liking, but she was still holding back. Craig came with possible consequences.

Chapter Ten

Nell walked toward her cottage having roamed through the cemetery to see if the blooms on each grave were still alive and well. Frost would take them at some point, and watering would come to a halt. While she loved autumn and the pure winter snows, she would miss the flowers she gifted to each recipient. There was something magnetic about taking care of, appreciating those who had come before. She never forgot that they had hopes, dreams, loves, and disappointments. And who could know if their soul-spirits lingered over their own stones, or over the stone of another? Where did the energy go when a body failed? Nell wasn't sure, but she decided young that since no one knew, she could believe what she wished, and her belief was that anything was possible.

As she walked close to the front door, Craig pulled into her driveway. Nell shielded her eyes from the brilliant setting sun to look up and smile as he turned his engine off and stepped from his car.

"Hey," he said. "I was thinking."

Nell laughed, "That is sometimes a dangerous thing to do."

He walked close to her. "No, no danger from me. I was wondering how you'd feel about going out for a meal with me, then we could come back here for another slice of that pumpkin pie. You're making more for Thanksgiving, right?"

Nell looked into his twinkling eyes. "Of course. But instead of going out for a bite tonight, how would you feel about minestrone soup and fresh bread from the bakery? That and pie would suffice, wouldn't it?"

Craig smiled. "I'd love it. Are you sure? I feel like I'm sponging on you."

Nell gestured that he should follow her into the cottage. "You've taken me out for dinner many times. It's my turn for a little payback. In fact, after tonight, you may take the rest of the pie home."

Craig looked at the pie on the island, wrapped lightly in tinfoil. "There was another. What happened to that one?"

Nell thought about telling him she'd devoured it for breakfast but decided on the truth. "I took it to a gentleman who works at the clinic. He's a widower, and I thought he'd like the pie."

Craig looked at her and nodded. He respected her kindness, her charming and beautiful nature. Nell was nothing like other women he'd known. She had an essence about her, a free spirit with the best intentions toward life in general.

"That was thoughtful of you. Anything I can do to

get things started?"

"Sure. I'll let you slice the bread." She passed him a sharp knife and cutting board. "There, and I'll give you the butter, too. I'll get the soup heated. I just made it this morning."

"How would you feel about me starting a fire for us to enjoy our pie next to?" he asked as the knife slid through the oval-shaped loaf.

"That's a great idea. Yes, we'll do that. In fact, I just picked up a trunkful of dry oak today. We can burn some of that."

Craig stopped slicing after cutting four pieces. "Could I get the wood out of your trunk for you?"

"I already did that. It's stacked in the corner by the hearth. It's part of my exercise routine, hauling wood for the hearth and water for the graves." Nell smiled as she placed two bowls on the island along with napkins and spoons. "Here we are, nice and hot. Beware."

Craig leaned toward the bowl and sighed. "Oh, this smells incredible. Your mom or grandmom again?"

"Nope. My mother, from what I remember, didn't make soup. I happen to love it, so I found this recipe online. I've made it half a dozen times for myself. It's especially good on a crisp day."

Craig reached for his spoon and carefully lifted the steaming mixture to his mouth. "This is incredible. The tomato soup we had last night, that was good, too."

Nell swallowed a spoonful of soup and smiled. "I

110

can't take credit for that – it came from a can. I like it enough to skip trying to make that from scratch. It's fun to experiment though. I like taking a recipe and adding my own touch here and there. This recipe was perfect, no need for anything more. I just followed it as directed."

Craig sat back a bit on his seat and looked at this amazing, pretty blonde who liked to cook and care for all souls – both living and dead. He couldn't help thinking how perfect she was.

With their soup and bread consumed, Nell ran water into their bowls, put the remainder of the soup away along with the butter, then heated coffee to go with their pie while Craig went to start the fire.

Warm mugs embraced by their hands, they sat close to the hearth as the blaze began to crackle and turn the flames from tangerine to blue then back to gold and particles of upward floating sparks. They sat staring at the flickering light, each of them silently appreciating being together.

"It kind of reminds me of the stars," he said. "Little flecks of light, absolutely mesmerizing."

Nell looked dreamily into the hearth, took a sip of her coffee and thought how imaginative and sweet this companion was. She was glad to know him, happy to have him in her life.

"So," he said as he finished his pie and took a swallow of coffee, "when should we shop for

Thanksgiving dinner? And, other than pie, what will we have for dessert?"

Nell laughed. "Two desserts? For just the two of us? Let's see. What do you like to have on Thanksgiving? Did you have a favorite sweet when you were growing up?"

Craig thought for a moment then smiled. "Yeah, chocolate cake, or really good brownies."

Nell laughed again. "We can definitely do the brownies, I have a good family recipe."

"Sounds perfect!"

"Okay then, we can shop for everything a few days ahead. You don't have any allergies, do you? For the stuffing I use bakery bread crumbs, roasted chestnuts, celery, a little finely chopped onion, and a handful of ground cranberries."

Craig looked at Nell and wondered how he'd been fortunate enough to find her. "I'm getting hungry all over again," he said. "And, no allergies. So should we shop the previous Saturday?"

Nell smiled, her face aglow from the flames just a few feet away. "That Saturday would work, yes."

When he left that evening, Nell let his lips meet hers. She felt an attachment to him that she'd never known before with anyone. He wasn't pushy, he gave her space to breathe, and he appreciated how she lived – at least what he knew of how she lived. They shared so much, from star-gazing to loving the simplicity of her little abode. How ironic, she thought, to have met someone with the same last name, who also hails from the West, and who seems like he'd be a perfect match in many ways. All but one.

When she heard his car crunching along her half-circle driveway and then pulling away, she leaned against the locked door, her eyes on the now nearly darkened hearth. How different everything would be if he hadn't had the affiliation with NAPS.

Nell walked to the kitchen window where she'd left the glass star he'd given to her. She picked it up in her hands and felt it grow warm with her own body energy. She held it to her heart, to her lips, then she took it to her bedroom where she placed it on her nightstand. She changed into pajamas then walked back to the kitchen where she washed their dishes and left them in the drainer to dry overnight. Quietly she opened the door to the little animal recovery unit and checked on the rabbit. She was doing well, the bandage secure. In a few days Nell would be taking her back for a check-up with Dr. Hill and, if all was well as she suspected, this little one would be returned to the wild.

Back in her parlor, Nell sat down with her book and pulled the six-inch chain on the floor lamp illuminating the pages. With the afghan on her lap, she read for an hour, closed the novel, poured herself a glass of water from the faucet, then went to her room.

Again, the night sky drew her in. The stars were

dependably there, and Nell reached for her gift from Craig. With the star in her left hand she reached to turn off the bedside light before slipping under the covers. She slept with the star clutched in her hands close to her heart.

***

She opened her eyes to a glimmer of sun seeping through her window and onto her bed quilt. Nell's thoughts were joyful thinking of the coming holidays, the first to be spent with Craig. If this is all I have, she thought, it will be mine alone forever. No one can take this memory we're about to create, no one will ever cause me to forget how I feel at this moment.

After changing from her pajamas to warm slacks and a dark green sweater, Nell slipped her feet into slippers and made her way to check on the rabbit. She was sitting still as though waiting for something good to nibble on. Nell went back into the kitchen and took bits of kale, part of a carrot, and seven blueberries to the rabbit, adding more timothy hay to her stash. Nell watched her for a few minutes, sorry that she would soon be leaving to hopefully reunite with family and friends in Dr. Hill's meadow-like back yard. And then Nell wondered what else would be living in that back room before long. There was no doubt, at some point there would be some needy little creature, but likely not until spring.

By noon Nell decided that since she'd managed to

forget about breakfast, she'd first make coffee then she'd have French toast with butter and genuine maple syrup, a gift from Dr. Hill and his wife. At her island, she sat with her food and bet herself that Craig would love this as much as she did. They had this other thing in common, good food.

For the remainder of her daylight hours, Nell decided to finish painting the autumn scene she'd started the day before, a simple maple against a three-rail fence, a meadow and hills in the distance. With the final stroke, she looked at her art work and decided that just maybe it could be framed and given to Craig at Christmas. She liked the thought. She wanted to believe it could be.

With her paints put away at dusk, she once again checked in on the rabbit then decided to make herself a light supper. The three days had been just what she'd needed – slow-paced, a nice time to unwind from a couple of difficult days at work. Nell took each patient's issue personally, as though these little pets were part of her. And while she thought often of getting herself a cat or dog, or two of each, Mrs. Olden still hadn't decided if she was moving to her daughter's house or not, and since the granddaughter was allergic, Nell would end up with the cat.

By seven o'clock it was dark outside and Nell decided another fire in the hearth was exactly what she wanted. She would keep TV on low for company but the book she was reading would be in her lap. When the phone rang, Nell was startled having fallen asleep.

"Hey," Craig said, "how was your day?"

Nell sat back in her chair and smiled to herself. "It was very good. How was yours?"

"Busy. I had two conference calls, one to Europe, one to Hawaii, totally different time zones, but at least the same topic. I thought about you though. Did you think about me?"

Nell laughed. "Um, let me think. Well, maybe for a moment or two."

Craig laughed. "I guess that's the response I deserve for having the audacity to inquire."

Nell sank back into her chair and watched the leaping flames in the hearth.

"Have you eaten yet? I'm starved, we could go for a bite."

"Thank you, but I made myself a sandwich and tea for supper. Don't you have anything to eat in your apartment?"

"Actually, I do. I have a loaf of white bread from the bakery beneath me and I have two varieties of cheese. So I think I'll tackle a grilled cheese the way you make them. Butter in the pan, not on the bread, right?"

"Either way works, but I tend to put it in the pan. Just remember, don't make the sandwich swim. You need the pan nice and hot, and you might need to turn it several times so as not to scorch it. Golden brown is what you want, and nicely melted cheese."

"Okay, I think I can handle that. Thanks. So, when can we get together? Are you working tomorrow?"

"Yes, tomorrow, but not the weekend. Any interest in going apple picking?"

"Sure, but are there still apples to pick?"

"Some," Nell said. "Most are harvested by now, but even so, they're plentiful at the farm stands and I'd love to get a bunch, or a bushel I should say. I thought I'd make a couple of apple pies, and maybe some homemade applesauce. If I get apples on Saturday, I can cook with them on Sunday."

"Can I come and play at your house Sunday, too?" he asked.

Nell grinned. "I think you could do that. I could put you to work peeling apples. I have this little apparatus that you clamp the apple into. You turn the handle and voila, the apple is peeled. I'll show you how to do it."

"Can't wait," he said and she knew he was sincere. "I'll have good company and apple pie, so all will be well. Let me know if I can bring anything to contribute. Other than my apple-peeling muscles, of course."

Nell laughed so hard that she had tears and needed a moment before she could reply. "I was actually thinking of making corn chowder. Do you like that? If so, you could bring a nice loaf of bread to go with it,

117

and we could have apple pie for dessert."

"That all sounds perfect. Do you like a little zip? I'm really hooked on this jalapeño cheddar bread right now, and I bet it would pair perfectly with corn chowder."

"Absolutely."

Craig paused for a moment then confessed, "I love the casual way you live. Growing up, Sunday was a massive dinner with all the fixings. It looked like my mom never stopped, then we ate it all in about thirty minutes."

"It was like that for me, too," she said. "Big dinners, and often guests who dropped in just at the right time, lots of food, lots of dishes. I liked the visitors, but I kind of decided that when I was grown up, I'd do things differently."

"I wonder if all people our age are thinking the same, less fuss."

Nell glanced around the room where she sat, the flickering flames casting shadows and warm light against the walls and furniture. "Maybe some, but I had friends in California who were very traditional about their homes and their food preparations. I guess it's the individual choice."

"I suppose so. Well, I guess I'll go experiment in the kitchen and I'll plan to see you Saturday for the apple hunt."

"Okay, what time?"

"How about ten? It's supposed to be good weather, sunny and bright."

"Sounds wonderful," Nell said. "See you Saturday morning."

Having spent the remainder of the evening reading, Nell finished her book and held it to her heart. The characters were riveting, the plot spell-binding. She would miss those people, but she was glad that everything had worked out well for the characters. If only her life could be that perfect.

She stood slipping the book onto the shelf next to her chair then shut off the TV and reading lamp. From there she went in to see the rabbit, told her she'd be taking a ride with her the next day to see Dr. Hill, and then she went to her room. In pajamas and slippers, she sat on the edge of her bed and reached to turn off the light. The stars were bright in the clear sky. She had wondered so often as a child how many others had their eyes to the heavens just at the exact time as she. It was an irresistibly free show like no other.

Chapter Eleven

It had been requested by Dr. Hill that his rabbit friend be brought to him for release in his yard early Saturday morning. At seven-thirty, Nell stopped at his home, the rabbit and carrier taken to the doctor's backyard. He and his wife met Nell there and transferred the frightened animal into a large cage where she would spend the weekend. On Monday, the plan was to examine her thoroughly, remove the bandage, then open the cage and set her free. It was, Dr. Hill thought, the kindest way to release, giving the animal time to adjust. Nell felt tears as she left the Hill home and headed back to her own cottage. There, she made coffee and then cleaned out the cage where the bunny had spent time in recovery. While Nell felt a bit sad, she also understood and accepted that this was the best situation for the rabbit. It was never easy letting go.

At just before ten, Craig pulled into the driveway and was about to knock when Nell opened the door. "Coffee before we go?" she asked.

"I never say no to coffee. I see you're dressed appropriately for our excursion. Nice warm sweater, sensible shoes."

Nell laughed as she turned toward the kitchen to pour two coffees. "You sound like my mother – always aware of keeping the body warm and wearing the right footgear."

Craig smiled as he pulled out his stool from the island. "I think your family and I will get along just fine."

Nell wasn't sure what he meant by that remark, but she sat down with their mugs of coffee and didn't ask questions.

"So, where are you thinking we should head toward for the best apples?" he asked.

Nell thought for a moment and then said, "Bellowton maybe, or just beyond. It's a great day for a little ride."

Craig nodded. "That it is. I love little jaunts, and to search out unfamiliar places to me is an interesting adventure. "I've been to Bellowton a few times, but never further. It's kind of crazy, but I feel like this area was always waiting for me to show up. I've lived all over the world and never felt this attachment to a place before now."

Nell agreed. "I felt the same way when I arrived here in my rented car. There was this magnetism beckoning me to stay. It didn't take any time at all to convince me. I bought a car, moved in, and took over what my grandfather had been doing as caretaker. It came natural, and then I was lucky enough to find a job just three miles away with Dr. Hill. It's perfect."

Craig had it on the tip of his tongue to say that *she* was perfect, but he held his voice and just nodded in agreement. "So, let me get this straight, today we're picking apples, or buying them, and tomorrow we're making pies and applesauce?"

Nell stood, rinsed her cup then reached for his as he finished the last gulp. "That's the plan. Tomorrow you can learn how to properly make a pie and applesauce."

Their ride through twisting roads led them to scenic meadows and more hills, the bright sun adding to the colors in the foliage. Nell would point to a flame-red maple, Craig would comment on a cluster of oaks.

When they found a pick-your-own apple farm, they were told that most of the fruit was down and in bushels, ready to take home. They looked at one another and at the same time said, "Next year, earlier."

They carried their large basket to the car, and then Nell pulled a cider doughnut from a bag. She broke it in half and they each enjoyed the treat as they continued their ride.

After a few minutes more of taking in the scenic views, Nell said, "There's a café not far from here. How about I treat you to lunch? You've been such a willing participant about helping with the apples."

"Well, I expect to benefit from this apple hunt with a pie of my own to take home. But, sure, I could eat. That half a donut reminded me how hungry I am."

122

"It's coming up just on the left, after the next bend," Nell said. "Shaugnessy's Café. It's home cooking and they prepare what they choose, but everything's good."

Craig pulled the car close to the café's front door and turned off the motor. "It's a homey looking little place. You've been here before then?"

"Several times for take-out, but I've never eaten inside. I pull out of my driveway and head to the left most often for work and town, but it's nice to head right and find a more country atmosphere. I think you'll like it. They make great Irish soups and stews."

Craig laughed. "I suppose that makes sense with a name like Shaughnessy. You and I will fit right in with our last name."

Seated inside at a table covered in a green and white checked cloth, they looked at the menu.

Nell told Craig, "Everything I've sampled has been excellent. Today I'm having potato Stew. It's made with cream and butter, caramelized onions, mushrooms, and potatoes of course. It's so good."

Craig ordered the same. The jovial waitress brought them each a warm biscuit and butter, a pot of Irish tea, and within minutes, their stew was served. Craig took a bite and shook his head side to side. "Oh boy, this is fantastic."

Nell smiled at him and began to take small portions into her mouth. It was still steaming yet impossible to wait on its cooling.

"What are we doing tonight?" he asked as he patted his lips clean with a linen napkin.

"I didn't know we were doing *anything* tonight," she said.

"Do you have plans?"

"No. Do you have something in mind?"

Craig raised his eyebrows. "I was thinking that if we dressed warm enough we could go to Bearstone for the stars again. It may be the last time before winter. I hear snow is popular up there."

Nell agreed it would be perfect timing. "I'd love that. It was wonderful to be up there with the constellations so visible. Yes, let's go. Maybe around eight when it's nice and dark?"

"Sounds good to me. So we'll meander through these fabulous back roads a bit longer and then I'll take you and your apples home. I'll catch up on some laundry and errands, then I'll see you later. Dinner?"

Nell shook her head. "Not for me. I might have one of these crisp apples before we go. That potato stew was filling, more than enough for a middle of the day meal."

Craig agreed and said he'd grab a piece of fruit or a slice of toast with peanut butter. His Irish luncheon was huge. "Okay, we'll do eight o'clock, and I think we're in for a dazzling night. And this time we'll know to dress warm."

At home, Nell walked into the back room out of

habit, then she thought how lonely it seemed in that empty space, with the rabbit adjusting back to life in the meadow. That room had now provided respite to squirrels, a bird, one chipmunk, and one rabbit. She knew there would be more and that it would go on and on in an endless parade of creatures that needed help. No matter what, she would supply that help. For now, she didn't concern herself with Craig discovering her secret. She wasn't sure what she would do if he ever observed and uncovered her camouflaged existence. Maybe he would rethink what his feelings were for her. Maybe he'd report her. Maybe he wouldn't.

At just after eight, Craig showed up at Nell's cottage. Finishing a cup of hot coffee she asked if he'd like one before braving the chill at Bearstone. "I had one just before I left my place. Thank you, though. I'm ready if you are. I have my scarf, my gloves, and I can see you're also well prepared."

Nell reached for her hip length coat, scarf, gloves, and then she pulled on a hat over her blonde locks.

Craig looked at her and smiled as he reached for her hand. "You look about four years old with that pom-pom on your hat," he teased.

Nell nodded. "Sometimes I feel about four. I kind of like it."

***

They took the flashlights from Craig's car and started up the path to the star-gazing area. They

125

weren't the only spectators there. At least thirty people were gathered, all with their eyes to the sky. They were greeted by many, and then they found the perfect perch, a fallen tree with enough room for eight humans to sit. When a ninth gentleman came along and indicated he'd like to join them, everyone pushed over, placing Craig and Nell close together. The heat from his left hip radiated against her right, then she felt his left arm pulling her closer. It was nice, warmer, and a move not without affection.

Her heart beating faster than she'd recalled it ever pulsing before, Nell tried to concentrate on finding Orion and the Little Dipper. She found what she hoped for, including the closeness to Craig.

"Just to remind all you good folks," an elderly woman said to the group at just about ten o'clock, "this is it, our last time this year on Bearstone. They're closing everything except the parking lot in preparation for winter. However, come spring we'll gather again for the sky show. Have good holidays everyone. See you next year."

Nell and Craig got up and he took her hand. They were among the youngest in the group and took a bit of good-natured teasing from an older fellow. "Hope it didn't spoil your evening finding a bunch of us up here tonight," he said with a big smile as he wrapped his arm around the woman next to him. "This is where I proposed to my wife more than fifty years ago."

Everyone applauded and commented on the romantic gesture. Nell felt Craig squeeze her hand and was glad it was too dark to detect her flushed face. Being close to him was magnetic. Not knowing what would happen next terrified her.

At the front door to the cottage, Nell placed the key in the lock. She turned to ask if he'd like a coffee or a hot cocoa, but there was no time for the words to leave her lips. He was there, kissing her, pulling her so close that she didn't know where she ended and he began. When he finally released her enough to breathe, they looked into one another's eyes. She was going to ask him again about the coffee or cocoa, but instead their lips met again. After those two passionate kisses, Nell decided it was probably best to not invite him in.

"I loved today," he said as he took her hands. "What time should I be here tomorrow?"

"How about noon? I know that plan was for me to make us some corn chowder, but since we had the potato stew today, would you prefer bruschetta?"

"It just happens I love both corn chowder and bruschetta. It's your choice," he said. "See you at noon." He leaned forward for another light kiss then turned toward his car.

Nell watched him walk away from her. She listened to the familiar purr of his engine and the crunching gravel beneath his car's tires. She waved goodbye then entered the cottage. She leaned against the inside of the door and closed her eyes, then opened them and looked toward the darkened hearth. Too late for a fire, yet that's exactly what she would have liked. The warmth and the glow would have been comforting after a few chilly hours on the side of Bearstone.

In the kitchen she made herself a cup of lemon-ginger tea and sat down with it at the island. She made a list of what she wanted to do with the apples. Four pies, one for Dr. and Mrs. Hill, one for Benjamin, her friend at the clinic, freeze one for Thanksgiving dessert, and one for Craig to take home. She smiled at the thought of him leaving with his own pie. Then she would cook up the remaining apples for applesauce, adding sugar and cinnamon. The cottage was going to smell distinctively enticing. She added to her list that for tomorrow's lunch with Craig, she would make both corn chowder and bruschetta in the morning. Whatever they didn't consume on Sunday could be Monday's lunch or supper.

After a warm shower, Nell changed into pajamas and put heavy socks on her feet. It was close to midnight, but she was wired after having been on a kiss-me-goodnight date with Craig and for what their day would be like cooking together in just about twelve hours.

She prepared diced tomatoes and onions then took two bags of corn niblets from her freezer in preparation for the chowder. She looked at what she'd assembled on the island and then decided to dice two large potatoes and pre-cook them before she went to bed. Delicious smells mixed with anticipation of what the next day would bring, filled her soul. After fifteen minutes she tested the potatoes for tenderness and turned them off. She finished her tea, turned out the light over the island, then went to her room and slept.

Chapter Twelve

When Nell opened her eyes on Sunday morning, she instantly looked forward to what she was doing on that bright sunny day. She loved to cook, and she loved Craig. Realizing that admission, Nell felt stunned. She'd had a few crushes throughout her years, but she'd never been *in love*. Yet here it was, loud and stomping through her veins. She was entranced by his charm and all they shared.

A fresh cup of coffee in her hands, she decided on a crisp apple for breakfast, then set about further preparations for the chowder and bruschetta. Choices, she would offer him choices.

She smiled as she worked. Next Nell assembled the pie crust ingredients. She had her mother's recipe for the best, made by adding a small amount of ginger ale for moisture. Four pies with two crusts was going to be a fair amount of dough. She took a wooden spoon and large bowl from the cupboard and began.

Before she realized the time, there was a knock on the door. In her casual pajama wear, she opened the front entrance to Craig. He looked at her from head to toe and smiled.

130

"I'm sorry. Time got away from me," she said. "I'd planned to change into jeans and a shirt."

"You look perfectly fine to me," he said. "And, wow, it smells fantastic in here! You made chowder?"

Nell grinned as he stepped inside. She closed the door and admitted, "I made both chowder and bruschetta actually. We'll have leftovers for tomorrow."

"Don't bet on leftovers. I'm starved."

Together they walked to the kitchen. "There's fresh coffee. How about if you pour yourself some while I change, and then we can have lunch before we get started on the apples?"

Craig nodded and made his way to the French press. He poured himself a mug of coffee then walked around the kitchen, sipping while he waited for Nell to return. When she did, he took in her snug jeans and bright red shirt with sleeves rolled up to her elbows. Her blonde locks back in a ponytail, she looked like a teenager.

"So," she said, "what will it be? Chowder or bruschetta?"

Craig cocked his head in thought for a moment then said, "Corn chowder. Maybe later we can have bruschetta by the fire followed by apple pie."

Nell laughed. "As long as we make sure to add vanilla ice cream on the pie."

"You have ice cream?"

Nell smiled and nodded. "I do."

After a satisfyingly delicious lunch, Nell set the apple peeler before Craig, who was a quick study. She formed the dough into pie crusts and then together they sliced the apples for the four pies. He watched as she measured cinnamon, sugar, and a touch of nutmeg then mixed them in with the filling. After pinching the top crust edges and placing the pies in the oven to bake, they set about peeling and cutting another thirty apples for the sauce. The kitchen was saturated with the sweet promise of a tasty dessert.

"You know what I think?" Craig asked as he washed his hands in the kitchen sink.

Nell poured each of them another cup of coffee. "What?"

"I think we should add another bedroom or two, and probably a second bathroom to this place." Craig picked up a towel and dried his hands. He leaned his back against the counter and stared into her eyes.

Nell laughed. "Does my skill in the kitchen imply I want to open a bed and breakfast?"

"No."

Nell noticed his serious expression and waited for more. When he didn't offer further explanation, she asked, "Okay, what were you implying then?"

"I thought we could get married. We're perfect together. Don't you agree?"

Nell looked bewildered. "Married? We've known each other maybe six months. We've only been on a few dates. And you think we're ready for a permanent relationship?"

"Aren't we?"

"Good Lord, you can't be serious." She went to the stove and stirred the steaming applesauce.

"But I am." He put his hands on her shoulders and turned her toward him. "Nell, I knew the first time I met you, standing at the front door of this place, that you had captured my heart."

Their eyes held one another and after neither of them spoke for several minutes he finally said, "I thought you might feel something similar. Am I off on this, should I go?"

Nell looked into his eyes, took his hands in hers, and smiled. "No, you shouldn't go. Please stay. Having you in my life has opened up a beautiful new path. I just think we need a little more time before we decide to walk down the aisle. There's still so much we don't know about each other."

After a few moments of thought he looked at her. "I don't want to scare you away, Nell. I know everything I need to about you, but if you want me to stay, if there are questions you still need answered, if there's any chance you feel the same way about me, then I'm not going anywhere."

"You can't frighten me away. You're not a bear," she teased, trying to lighten the mood. "And besides, we're having good food then warm pie and ice cream shortly. You wouldn't want to miss that, would you?"

Craig half smiled as he looked toward the floor then at Nell. Squeezing her hands, he said, "I don't want to miss *anything* with you."

They stood holding hands quietly, eyes locked. When the apple sauce started to bubble, Nell let go to stir it. Craig didn't move.

"Would you like more chowder or some bruschetta? Or the pies should be ready soon."

Craig nodded. "Life's uncertain. We should eat dessert first. Pie with ice cream would be first rate."

"Okay. If you start a fire going in the hearth, I can bring it in there for us. More coffee?"

"Sure, that sounds good."

When he walked into the parlor, Nell closed her eyes for a moment and swallowed. He'd surprised her enormously with his suggestion that they share the cottage in marriage. The idea was appealing, except for her little wild patients. What would he say about them living under his roof with a caretaker who wasn't licensed? She didn't want to be licensed – she knew how NAPS could walk up to the door whenever they pleased, and they could also bring you more animals than you were prepared for. Nell liked helping what she could on her own terms. And with the help and confidence of Dr. Hill, she could manage that just fine.

She pulled the pies from the oven and turned the stovetop off, carefully moving the large pot of applesauce to an unused burner. With fresh coffee brewing in the press, she carefully sliced into one of the steaming pies, cutting each of them a generous piece, then scooped ice cream on top. She added forks and napkins to the tray, then the two new cups of coffee and the dishes of pie ala mode.

Nell set the tray before a now blazing hearth, and they sat down opposite one another with their dessert and coffee.

"That pie was the best, Nell," Craig said as he sat back with his coffee. "I completely enjoyed being part of the process, and the results are amazing. The applesauce smells really good too."

"It was fun. Thank you for helping. We were a decent team, both yesterday and today."

Craig looked at her and decided to say nothing. He'd already overwhelmed her with a lopsided proposal. This wasn't something he could rush, but she wanted him to stay, and that was enough for now.

They both gazed at the fire, the leaping flames reaching upward, the logs crackling in the dim light of early evening.

"I should probably get going," he said as he stood.

"Okay, but hold on. I'll get your pie wrapped. Maybe you'll warm a piece for breakfast."

"I definitely will," he said as he walked close to the hearth.

Nell returned to the parlor with a basket that held a

container of chowder, bruschetta, and the pie. She held it toward him and said, "Choices."

He accepted the basket and looked at her beautiful face. "This was a really special day."

Nell nodded. "Yes, it was. And Thanksgiving will be here before we know it. Are we still planning to shop together the Saturday before? And then maybe that Wednesday, if you're up for it, we can start the preparations."

"I'm in. But I'd like to see you before that if you're available."

Nell smiled. "I'd like that. I work tomorrow until four, and the same for Tuesday. Then I'll have a couple of days off."

"Maybe we could go find some pumpkins on Wednesday?"

"That sounds fun. Okay, Wednesday it is."

"Okay," he said as he turned toward the door. He put the basket down on the floor as he slipped his arms into his jacket then picked it back up. He thought about a goodbye kiss, but he decided not to push himself on her, he'd already done that a little too well.

Nell stood, wishing he had left her with a kiss.

Monday and Tuesday were busy days at the clinic, leaving Nell to get home after dark. On Tuesday, Craig called to ask if she wanted to grab a little dinner out.

"After being out at the clinic the past two days, I think I'd rather stay in. But I still have chowder and bruschetta left. If you want to come here, we could enjoy them by the fire."

"You don't have to invite me twice. I'll be there in an hour."

Nell went and took a shower, changed, then transferred the chowder to a pan so it could be reheated.

Craig was punctual, as always. He arrived with a bottle of wine in hand, and they spent their evening together, eating and sharing childhood and teen years stories. They had been similar children, aware of their good lives.

***

On the Wednesday evening before Thanksgiving, they sorted through the vegetables and dry goods. Nell smiled at the abundance as Craig took inventory to make sure they had all that was needed.

"I can't believe it's tomorrow," he said. "So, when do we start the big cook-off? Tomorrow morning?"

Nell nodded. "Yes, tonight we'll get the vegetables chopped, the chestnuts roasted, and we'll keep a modest list to keep us on track. And I have a question – how do you feel about chocolate cream pie for dessert? It's not traditional, but I could make one tomorrow morning easily. Or we can stick to the original plan – chocolate cake or brownies."

"You are spoiling me," Craig began. "While all of the above sounds terrific, I haven't had chocolate cream pie in forever."

"Settled," Nell said. "I'll make that in the morning. I'm just going into work long enough to give two cats some fluids and then their owners are picking them up to take them home for Thanksgiving."

"I suppose," Craig said, "some of them end up at the clinic over holidays."

"That's true, but Dr. Hill gets his patients home if it's at all possible. And not too many people know, but out in the back of the clinic there's a small apartment. A woman, Millie, lives there. She isn't a tech, but she's a fabulous addition to the staff. She's grateful for a place to live, and Dr. Hill is grateful that if there was a fire or other danger, Millie would be on site to call for help. She makes sure the patients are fed and have water, and she keeps an eye on them. That means the world to all of us – the animals are never left on their own."

"Your boss sounds like a pretty cool guy. I like that the animals are safe there."

Nell looked appreciatively at Craig. He cared about the little lives at the clinic. Now if she could only be brave enough to find out what he'd think of her nurturing the sweet souls from the meadows as well.

When he left to go back to his apartment that evening, Nell thought about him and wished she could think their future was more positive. She could not accept denying shelter and treatment to her small woodland friends, not even for Craig. So was this connection they were presently enjoying doomed to fail? Nell decided that even if it was, for the time being she would enjoy and remember the wonder of knowing and caring for a man like him. One step at a time – and for now, she was going to love every moment of the holidays.

Nell took a last look around the kitchen before organizing what she needed for the chocolate cream pie, then she took a deep breath and walked to her room where she changed into pajamas and climbed into bed beneath fresh linens and a warm quilt. With the nightstand light out, she closed her eyes then opened them again for a last look toward the sky. They were there, all those fascinating little lights sparkling as though they understood precisely how much joy they delivered.

Tomorrow morning, she murmured to the stars. Craig and I will fuss about in the kitchen, the two of us side by side, and then our Thanksgiving. This is going to be crazy wonderful.

Chapter Thirteen

Having spent her first hour of the day taking sips of freshly brewed coffee while making the chocolate cream pie, Nell felt elated for the later part of the day, when Craig would be there to put his cooking abilities to work.

With the pie finished, except for the final touch, a mountain of fresh whipped cream, Nell dressed in her clinic attire and headed out. As she steered her car into town, she realized that this was more than a career. It was a service to be there for the frightened and ill little ones who needed the gentle touch, the soft whispers. The only bad part was when one couldn't recover. Luckily, that wasn't the case right now.

With zero animals left to tend for the holiday, Nell drove home and felt as though her entire being was smiling with the prospect of preparing an enticing meal with Craig. She'd never done that before. In California it was her mother and grandmother at the helm, with Nell peeling potatoes or cutting green beans. Her first year in Connecticut she let Thanksgiving slide by as she filled in at the clinic then went home to a sandwich and tea. She'd told her parents that evening that she had enjoyed a huge meal with friends. They'd have been horrified with her having a sandwich alone.

Nell showered and changed into relaxing attire. As she headed toward the kitchen, the phone rang.

"Hello there," Craig began. "I just wanted to know if we need anything else we might have forgotten."

Nell thought for a moment. "Any chance you have some butter? Otherwise, I think we're set."

"I just happen to have some in the fridge. I'll bring it with me. See you soon."

When he arrived with a huge white chrysanthemum, Nell smiled and reached for the plant. "Wow, this is gorgeous."

"I thought it would be festive for our table and then it could sit on your front step next to your pumpkins. They still look great, but I was figuring the squirrels would have nibbled at them by now."

Nell smiled. "Well, I have a little secret. I rub cooking oil on the pumpkins. It discourages little teeth, and it also makes the pumpkins glisten."

He watched as Nell placed the plant on a footstool in the parlor. "Maybe it's a little bit of overkill," he said as he rubbed his chin. "It was just so impressive at the greenhouse."

Nell laughed. "It's absolutely perfect. I love it. But if we set it on the table, we might not be able to see across to one another."

Craig laughed then followed her into the kitchen.

He washed his hands as she set their places with dishes, napkins, forks, and wine glasses.

"Would you like something to drink?" Nell asked.

Craig sat down and appraised the array of pre-dinner offerings – apple sauce, a tray of assorted nuts garnished with grapes, crackers and cheese. "Coffee?"

"Sure. Coming right up." Nell poured the brew from the French press into a mug for him then topped off her own cup.

He thanked her, took a sip, and began to help himself to the cheese and crackers. Nell did the same. They were silent as they enjoyed the mix of healthy snacks.

"This is so good," Nell said, dabbing with a napkin at grape juice on her chin. "I was thinking this morning though that sometime soon I should get pizza. When I leave the clinic I'm usually so focused on getting home that I don't stop anywhere. I'll have to change that."

"Let me move in here with you and I'll change all that," Craig said as he chewed then swallowed a handful of peanuts.

Nell gave him a quick glance and he smiled. "No worry. Just kidding. So, should we begin making dinner? I'm not sure how long stuffed squash takes."

"It shouldn't be more than a couple of hours," she said. "I just need to clear some of this out of the way first so we have room to work."

Their food prep went just as Nell had planned. Her

142

time with Craig turned the day into joyful hours. Dinner had been delicious as planned, and they were pleasantly filled as they took a brief walk while the plates and utensils soaked in the sink.

After washing the dishes and putting the leftovers away, Nell challenged Craig to a game of Scrabble. After two games, they finally had room for dessert. By nine o'clock they were tired and ready to sit down with something hot to drink by the blazing hearth.

Craig took his usual spot on the sofa. "I think you tired me out. Not to mention your aggressive game manuevers."

Nell laughed as she sat across from him. "Yes, it's been a full day. And Scrabble was fun. I think we may have prepared enough food, though that we'll both have leftovers for a couple of days."

"Leftovers are the best part. So, what time should I be here tomorrow?" he asked with a smile. Nell smiled in return deciding to withhold a reply.

When they'd finished their drinks, Craig stood, rubbed his eyes, and walked toward where he'd left his jacket. He hesitated, but when she walked closer to him, he leaned in for a gentle kiss on her perfect lips. "I loved today. Best Thanksgiving ever. But don't tell my mother I said that."

Nell laughed as he pulled her close and kissed her again, then she watched as he moved to his car, slipped inside with a wave, and left.

She was in a daze, watching his taillights trail into the distance, when the phone rang. Her parents were both on the line to wish her a happy day and to see what she'd been up to.

***

Nell fell into her bed thinking of Craig. She may have beaten him at Scrabble, but sleep won against her.

When she woke in the morning the sun had strewn itself over her colorful quilt and she smiled for the new day that was about to begin. Every particle of that holiday had been ideal, and adding a stroll in the cemetery to wish a happy Thanksgiving to their grandfathers had been bliss in the crisp air.

The phone rang as Nell was pouring herself a cup of coffee, smiling when she saw that it was Craig.

"Good morning. I just wanted to thank you again for yesterday. It was, and I repeat – don't ever tell my mother I said this – the absolute best Thanksgiving I've ever had."

Nell laughed. "Agreed. Even though I have memories of wonderful holiday dinners with my family – my parents, my aunt and uncle, my grandparents – that I wouldn't trade for anything, yesterday was sensational."

"We did that, all by ourselves," Craig said, "and I hope we get to do it over and over for the next hundred years."

Nell was glad he was on the phone so he couldn't

see her blush. She glanced out the window, smiling.

"Am I scaring you away? Because that's definitely not my intention," he said.

Nell was quiet for a few moments. "We'd be so old," she teased, and then they both laughed. Nell wondered how she'd come to deserve such a delightful time. "I think we were both so tired last night that I forgot to send you home with food. Do you want to stop by in a little bit? I just made coffee."

"I will take every opportunity I can to see you. Any chance you want to go for a little drive? Maybe we can find a shop to browse in so I can get started with my Christmas shopping."

"Sold," Nell said.

Within an hour, Craig pulled into her driveway. Nell met him at the door with two containers of coffee in thermal mugs, and they got into the car for a joy ride. After being gone from mid-morning until early afternoon, and having explored a few shops and grabbing a pizza for lunch, they headed back to her cottage where she sent him home with three containers of food, one with chocolate cream pie.

On Saturday morning, Nell decided a nice grilled cheese would be perfect for breakfast. As she flipped the browned sandwich to the opposite side, the phone rang.

"Hey there," Craig said, "do you have any plans for this evening? I was thinking it would be fun to see a movie and have a bite to eat someplace?"

Nell didn't hesitate. "Yes to the movie, and yes to the bite out." To her heart she said yes to spending more time with Craig.

***

"I think," he said over dinner, "that we should talk about Christmas."

Nell looked up from her salad in anticipation. She'd been wondering what Christmas would entail but hadn't wanted to seem too anxious.

"You're staying here for the holidays, as am I, right?" he asked. When she nodded, he continued. "Can I invite myself to your home and we'll have dinner and the day together?"

Nell felt her abdomen constrict. He'd just asked what she hoped he would. "That sounds great. We'll have to decide what we want to eat. I'm thinking those brownies and chocolate cake that we delayed from Thanksgiving might be in order."

"Ah, you know me so well. Those sound perfect. I can just picture us eating them together by the twinkling tree lights. Did you have a tree last year?"

Nell nodded as she swallowed a sip of her drink. "I did, a real one, two feet high. I planted it in my back yard before the ground was frozen. I think I might be up for an artificial one this year though, a big one."

"I'm up for an artificial one, too. I like the idea of not taking a live tree and then tossing it two weeks later. That's settled then. We'll shop for a tree and we'll do Christmas together. Do you have ornaments?"

Nell raised her eyebrows and smiled. "Last year I used cardstock paper and cut out little white stars for my tree. I made one dozen, and with tiny white lights, it was nice."

Craig smiled at her. "Stars, eh? So, with a bigger tree, we'll need more stars. How about some evening soon we tree shop, then another night cut stars out?"

Nell's heart lurched with the prospect of having Craig to herself on her favorite of holidays. This was going to be unforgettable, no matter what the future might bring. "Yes," she said, "we'll cut stars by the fire with hot cocoa."

The following weekend they bought a six-foot tree and additional white lights. They cut fifty-four stars, some small, some three inches wide. They chose a place in the parlor for the tree to glimmer and then they sat down to admire the soft yet festive setting. Everything fell into place.

***

"I don't feel like I see nearly enough of you," he said one night in a phone call. "I've been really busy, too busy really, but I've had time to think about you. I can't wait to see you again."

Nell sat down with the phone in her hands and changed the subject. "Did you send anything to your parents?"

"Actually I sent them a massive poinsettia and a gift certificate for the whole family to go out to dinner at their favorite restaurant."

"That was a nice idea."

"What about you?" he asked. "Did you send gifts?"

Nell pulled her feet under her. "I did. I sent gifts to my parents and my aunt and uncle. And I was told a box was on its way to me as well. I love this time of year. It encompasses all the sweet memories of the past and thought for the future. By the way, we should decide on dinner for Christmas. I have an idea, but I'm not sure what you'll think."

"Tell me," he said. "Wait, let me guess. Star-shaped grilled cheese sandwiches?"

Nell laughed. "That's not a bad idea, but how about lasagna, salad, and really good bread?"

"And chocolate cake and brownies?"

"Of course," Nell responded.

"Perfect."

When their call ended, Nell made herself a cup of tea and sat by her glowing hearth. She wondered if anything in her lifetime had ever been anywhere near as perfect as this time with Craig. Already there was a light covering of snow on the ground and clinging to the bare trees, like frosting on a cake. It was as though everything was made new with the breathless blanket of white.

Nell couldn't help but wonder how her little squirrel

friends were faring in their first introduction to the cold. She left extra seed for them outside by her backyard tree, and she watched for them every morning, wishing she could provide them with warmth. Tender hearted, that's how her grandparents had described her, and Nell supposed that was true.

One week before Christmas Nell took her autumn watercolor painting to a frame store in town and selected a wide maple border to embrace Craig's gift. She made a gift tag from one of the stars they'd cut for the tree and wrapped the picture in layers of tissue and then red and white paper. With a large green bow on its top, she placed it beneath the tree. When she sat down to admire the celebratory glow of lights, she felt both excited and frightened. Losing Craig was the worst happening she could imagine.

Two days before Christmas Nell spent several hours baking Christmas sugar cookies in the shapes of angels, hearts, and stars. She happily made packages for everyone at the clinic and another for Craig. Each dozen was wrapped in red cellophane then tied with colorful bows. The cottage delightfully captured the aroma of cinnamon for at least a full day after the baking spree. With everything in order, including the ingredients for Christmas dinner, except for the bread which Craig would bring, Nell dusted the mantle and a small table then sat down as she allowed herself to dream. She could picture her life with Craig, and maybe with a baby or two, and definitely pets. She was beginning to think that the cat she might be adopting might not be happening. The owner still hadn't decided to move in with her daughter yet, but Nell was hopeful that soon she'd know definitively. Everything could be so incredibly perfect.

Chapter Fourteen

Christmas day always seemed magical to Nell. The atmosphere outside, whether in Connecticut or California, seemed to take on a luminous glow. As a child, she wished for snow, but in her state it was all about grass and flowers. She'd seen the movie *White Christmas* a dozen times, each time dreaming of seeing that white covering at some point. Now she was living it.

She had thought to make cinnamon buns for Christmas breakfast then ended up buying them at the bakery beneath Craig's apartment. She made coffee, took the butter from the refrigerator, then started to warm a single bun when there was a knock at her door. Startled and still in her pajamas, Nell tip-toed through the parlor and looked out through the window enough to see that her Christmas morning visitor was Craig.

"Merry Christmas," she said to him, opening the door, feeling a little shy about being in Christmas-themed pajamas.

Craig looked at her from head to toe. "You're adorable," he said with a big smile. "Merry Christmas to you. I decided to drop off the bread we're having with dinner, and I also picked up a plant. I wanted you to have it for the entire day."

Nell looked at the beautiful arrangement of white, pink, and red poinsettias growing together.

"It's gorgeous, thank you. And while you're here, would you like to have a cinnamon roll with coffee?"

Craig closed the door to the morning chill and left the plant near the hearth. "I would love a coffee and roll. Did you make them?"

Nell turned and walked toward the kitchen. "Nope, I thought about doing them, but I ended up picking them up at the bakery yesterday. I couldn't resist since I know how good they are."

Craig sat at the island as Nell poured him a mug of coffee and set a napkin, plate, and butter knife before him. She noticed his eyes surveying the kitchen then coming to rest on a red cellophane package tied with a bow. She followed his gaze and smiled as she took warmed cinnamon rolls and set them on the island. "That package," she said, "is for you. Sugar cookies, unless you don't care for cookies."

"Are you kidding? I love cookies. Thank you. You're just a little bundle of a baker, aren't you?"

Nell laughed then took a sip of her coffee. "I love to bake, more so than cooking, but cooking is kind of fun, too. What about you? Don't you prepare food for yourself?"

"Sure, if you count a peanut butter sandwich. I

suppose I could cook if I needed to, but having lived with a mother who could put together a good meal, a college cafeteria with pretty decent selections, and then the Army, I haven't had to do much about cooking. And now I have you."

Every time he alluded to their relationship, Nell felt stricken with modesty for what they meant to one another. Nell gave him a half smile then finished her coffee.

"What time should I show up later?"

"Any time you wish," Nell said. "I'll be here."

Craig was quiet for a few moments before he spoke. "Should I go and come back later, or should I just stay?"

Nell hadn't planned on him staying, but then why not? "You can stay. I'm sure my parents will call a bit later – they're certainly still sleeping given the time difference. What about *your* family?"

"I called last night. My gang usually has a Christmas Eve buffet for relatives and friends. I had the opportunity to talk to a few different people. They were having fun without me, can you imagine?"

Nell nodded and smiled. "My parents are away with my aunt and uncle. I think both my mom and dad miss their parents more than they say. The trip for the holidays gives them a chance to build new memories."

"They must miss you," he said.

Nell nodded. "They do, and I feel bad about that,

but it was time for me to fly the coop. When my grandfather left me this place to be caretaker for the cemetery, I was determined to give it a try. When I arrived here, I was instantly in awe of the place, a little house on Summers Bridge Road. It was like something out of a fairy tale. I can't imagine living anywhere else."

"I feel the same way."

Nell smiled and busied herself with cleaning some frosting from the countertop.

Earnestly trying not to seem pushy, Craig shifted back to the day at hand. "I'd love to stay and hang out with you. I have your gift in the car. I'll go grab that and then I'm all yours. You can tell me what you'd like me to do."

"To tell you the absolute truth, I was going to light the hearth and have a second cup of coffee before the tree. I just need to sprinkle parmesan on top of the lasagna a bit later. It doesn't take long to bake."

"Okay then. I like the sound of this. I'll get your present from the car then I'll move the poinsettia and start a fire. And another cup of coffee with you…wow, this day is coming together perfectly."

When he returned to the parlor, Nell quickly went to her room and changed into a pair of soft jersey slacks and a hip-length silk shirt in emerald green. She gave her hair a quick brushing then walked into the kitchen, poured two fresh coffees, and joined Craig in the parlor.

"This," he said as he squatted before the emerging flames, urging them to grasp onto oak logs from the kindling, "is definitely Heaven. I'm serious, Nell. I love this casual warmth you do so well."

Nell spotted a package beneath her tree, something long and narrow. She was filled with excitement to open it.

"This is nice, I agree," she said as she handed him his cup. "Dinner will be easy, about forty minutes for the lasagna to bake, and dessert is made. I'll just need to make a salad."

"Guess what?" Craig said. "I'm excellent at salads. I can make that later, and you can sit and relax as you watch me work. It's the least I can do. And I'll slice the bread I brought. I can do that, too."

Nell smiled at him. "And I'll let you. I'll set the table with your beautiful centerpiece at one end. If I place it in the center, I won't be able to see you."

They sipped coffee with their eyes traveling between the fire and the Christmas tree. It couldn't have been a more perfect setting.

Craig turned to look at Nell with a serious expression. It caught her off guard and she looked at him quizzically, her head cocked to one side. "Are you okay?" she asked.

Craig placed his cup down on the table next to him and then looked at Nell. "Sometimes I just get a little worried that I'm moving too fast for you. I'm tempted to say things that I feel, and I stop myself because I know how independent you are. If I ever say anything out of line, tell me. I don't want this to end, especially for saying something you're not ready for."

Nell was quiet at first, her eyes moving from Craig's handsome face to the flames, then back at him. "I think you're doing fine. We're two people with similarities, and we enjoy our time together. Let's just focus on that, especially on this wonderful Christmas day. In fact, you know what I was thinking? After we've had dinner, maybe we could take a walk in the snow. It's not deep, just a couple of inches, and it would be refreshing. What do you think?"

Craig nodded. "That sounds great. Then we can come back, have dessert, and open our gifts."

Nell looked from Craig to the package he'd left under the tree. "Yes, you have me curious about what you've brought. I've been silently guessing what it is. A branch perhaps? A long rolling pin so I can make really huge pie crusts? Or..."

"You're just going to have to wait," he said in a teasing voice. "And anyway, you haven't revealed what that other package with the big green bow is, or even who will be the recipient."

Nell squinted her eyes and bit down on her lower lip. "Hmm, I'm not sure I've decided." When she smiled at him, he knew.

Close to noon they'd finished their coffee at just about the time the fire was barely glowing. They moved to the kitchen and Nell preheated the oven then took out a salad bowl and all the ingredients. A cutting board and sharp knife were placed before Craig. He began by thinly slicing tomatoes, then lettuce, a cucumber, and a small portion of purple onion. He tossed the ingredients together then added a raspberry vinaigrette and a dash of black pepper. Nell laughed as she stood up and told him, "I haven't seen such moves since watching the Swedish chef on *The Muppets*."

Craig picked up a small piece of carrot that he'd just cut and threw it at her. Laughing, she caught it, popped it in her mouth, then said, "I'm going to put the lasagna in the oven then begin setting the table. Would you pour each of us a glass of wine, please?"

Craig washed his hands then heeded Nell's request. He watched as she took a red and white checkered tablecloth and napkins from a linen drawer, dishes from the kitchen cupboard, cutlery from a drawer, and turned an oval table in the living room into an appealing two-person setting. Her final touch was placing the poinsettia at one end.

Next Craig sliced the bread and placed it on a tray alongside the butter as Nell set out a small dish of Parmesan cheese. There was nothing more left to do other than enjoy the wine by a stoked fire.

"One small log should see us through from now

until we've finished dinner," he said. "Then we can take that walk you mentioned. I have to tell you, this is the very best Christmas in my entire world. I feel guilty for feeling that way because I had wonderful times at Christmas in California. But this place, being with you, it's all like a really terrific dream."

Nell nodded as she'd been thinking the same. "I'm enjoying it, too. I was alone here last year, and for someone who loves this holiday, it left me feeling a little melancholy. Everything this year is complete. I don't know how it could get any better. I'm really glad you're here."

When the timer went off Nell went to check on the lasagna then placed it on top of the stove to set. When she came back with the salad bowl, Craig got up and brought in the other items. With dinner arranged on the table and more wine poured, they sat down to an appetizing meal. Baked to perfection, the lasagna was sliced and served, the salad bread and butter passed from one to the other. Compliments flowed for each person's contribution as they sat back and enjoyed their festive surroundings.

"The fire is barely with us," Craig said. "It lasted just the right amount of time, until dinner's end. Even the hearth cooperated with our plans. Are you still wanting to take that walk you mentioned? Then we could come home and have dessert, presents, and a bright new fire. What do you think?"

Nell caught and loved that he'd said *home* rather than simply back.

"I'm ready. I'll just pull on my boots and a jacket."

"And a scarf, hat, and gloves," he suggested. "I have gloves in my coat, and I may have a scarf in the car."

Nell walked to the closet by the front door and handed Craig a wool scarf. "This was my grandfather's. It will keep you warm."

Craig wound the scarf around his neck once and then slipped his arms into his jacket, pulling gloves from the pockets. He watched as she moved her feet from shoes to boots then helped her into her winter attire. The temptation was there to put his arms around Nell and pull her close. He decided it wasn't a move he should make at that moment. This girl was worth assessing every move, every comment carefully.

It was after three when they left the house and shuddered as they breathed in the frosty air. The sun was already planning its descent beyond the hills, but it gifted them with golden touches to the glimmering snow. Each of them feasted their eyes to the dark branches glazed in white, the contrast creating what could have been a setting for a film.

"This place," Craig said as they entwined arms for their walk, "is like storybook material. I've been in many different parts of this world, but I can't imagine anything more perfect than Keltonville, Connecticut."

Nell smiled and agreed. "I won't ever leave here. This is home."

Craig thought about what he wanted to say next, choosing his words carefully. "What are your plans for the future?"

Nell looked up at him as they walked then looked off toward a collection of hills in the distance. "My plans are to live exactly as I do now. I have a home I love, a job I love, it's more than I could have imagined. And you?"

Craig looked around as they chose carefully where to step, avoiding slippery patches where ice had formed. "I'm here, and my plan is to stay. I'd never be able to duplicate what I have here anywhere else."

He thought about saying more then held back, allowing the beauty of the area to speak to each of them.

"I'm loving this," Nell said, "but I'm freezing. And besides, there could be bears out here. Let's turn back and build ourselves a wonderful fire. Dessert and presents are waiting."

"I'm with you," Craig said as they changed direction and headed back toward the cottage. "This was just what I needed though. We could make a nice hot pot of coffee when we get back inside."

"Or we could have hot cider," Nell said.

Craig smiled. "I should have picked up eggnog. My dad's stuff is potent, loaded with rum and bourbon."

"Both?" Nell asked as they reached her front door laughing.

"Oh yeah, that drink is killer material. No one ever left our house without a glow from Dad's concoction. My father's best friend used to claim that the drink was the result of draining our liquor cabinet. I'm betting they're having something equally as impressive right this minute."

"That reminds me," Nell said as she slipped her feet out of boots and left her jacket on a hanger, "I need to check my messages to see if my parents called. Either way, I think I'll give them a buzz. Thank goodness for cell phones – you can reach anyone anywhere. Would you start a fire? I won't be long."

Craig nodded and went about setting the logs in place, tucking kindling beneath them, and then he set the hearth aglow. He could hear Nell speaking softly to her parents and to someone else, an aunt he guessed. He could hear her laughing and he smiled at the girl who was brave enough to have traveled from one coast to another where she found a home and life waiting for her. He wanted to share all of that with Nell. They treasured the same things, shared the same values.

When she returned with the phone in her hand, Nell placed it down on a table and gave the hearth a long glance. "That's a perfect blaze," she said. "I'm at least six feet away and I can feel the heat."

Craig gave her a devilish grin. "Yes, but how do

161

you know it's from the fire and not me?"

"I think," Nell said smiling, "that you should behave yourself. It's Christmas after all."

"How's your family?" he asked.

"They're wonderful, sunning themselves by the sea with my aunt and uncle. It's not how I'd choose to spend the holidays, but it's what they enjoy."

"Speaking of the holidays," Craig began," I do believe it's Christmas day and we have yet to open our gifts. Shall we?"

"Yes," she agreed. "I just need something warm to drink first. Cider or coffee?"

"Whatever you're having," he replied.

When she came back with two steaming cups of cider, Nell placed them on the table then moved toward the tree. She lifted the gift for Craig and placed it in his hands. "I hope you'll like this."

He accepted the gift and assured her that he would love whatever she chose for him. Then he lifted the long, narrow package and placed it across Nell's arms. "This is magic. Just like you."

Nell held the lengthy piece and then went back to her seat near the hearth. Cautiously she untied the ribbon and then carefully removed the paper. She found a long rectangular box made of sturdy cardboard. Tempted to shake it, Nell smiled at Craig and then asked, "Is it fragile?"

He nodded, "A bit."

Proceeding to extract the gift from its container, she found that she was holding that magic he'd alluded to – Nell had her own telescope. Taking it from the box, she felt warm tears stream down her face onto her lips.

Craig walked near to her and knelt down. "Why the tears?" he asked gently. "I thought you'd love feeling closer to those stars of yours."

Nell wiped the tears away and looked from the gift to his face. "It's my best gift ever."

He moved to sit on the arm of her chair, his right arm draped over her shoulders. "I'm glad you like it. You are my keeper of the stars, Nell Miranda McGann, and while I don't want to be the cause of your tears, I do want you to possess the ability to see your night sky with more accuracy."

"We'll share it," she murmured and then wondered if they'd be together long enough to share anything at all come spring.

"There's a tri-pod for it in my car – it was too awkward for me to wrap. However, may I open *my* gift now?"

Nell nodded as he moved back to the sofa. She smiled at how carefully he untied the green bow then, without tearing the paper, he met layers of billowy white tissue and eventually the painting. At first glance he stopped, motionless, then removed the painting from its pretty wrapping. He stared at it, ran his fingers over the smooth maple frame, turned it around and around, then stared at the autumn scene.

Nell wondered if she'd assumed too much by giving it as a gift. Maybe she should have selected a warm sweater instead. It may, she thought, have been presumptuous to give him something she'd made.

When he looked at her, she could see that his eyes were glistening with tears.

"I don't even know if I can talk," he said. "Nell, this is so beautiful. It looks like the meadows along Summers Bridge Road. I can't find the words to explain how much I love this painting." He placed it down on the sofa next to him then stood and walked to her, pulling her to her feet. With an embrace tight yet tender they lingered for several minutes. "We're good," he said. "For Christmas we made each other cry."

Nell laughed but found more tears streaming down onto her face. She moved away enough to spread the moisture from her face to her hand and he did the same to himself. "I'm so glad you like it. Autumn seems to be your favorite season. I wanted to give you a forever memory of this place."

Craig looked at her, his arms now at her shoulders. "I love that painting more than anything else I've ever had as a gift, but believe me, Nell, I will never be anywhere but here. The forever memory you mentioned is going to be my life – my entire life."

"Goodness," she said drawing away from him by

just a few inches, "I think we've earned our dessert. I do have that chocolate cake and those brownies you claim to like so much. And we should make coffee."

After enjoying their dessert and coffee by the radiant hearth, Craig stood to take their dishes to the kitchen sink. "Don't go anywhere," he said. "I'll be right back."

Nell leaned back in her chair then upon his return was pulled forward as Craig led her about six feet to the sofa. Together they sat down, Nell a willing captive.

Wrapping his arms around her, he looked into her eyes and asked, "So, was this a merry Christmas for you?"

Nell looked at the fire and said, "Um, I might need to think about that before I reply." Then she leaned toward him with a kiss. "It was beyond merry. I feel absorbed by the holiday and by the company. I doubt anything could be more joyful than how we made this day."

Craig took the initiative to lean in for another kiss and then they sat quietly, their eyes on the hearth.

By close to midnight the fire was smoldering. Nell yawned discreetly and allowed her head to rest against his shoulder.

"Should I go home?" he asked.

Nell smiled with her eyes closed. "I suppose at some point you should."

Craig pulled her closer. "I could stay."

Nell opened her eyes and realized how completely intense she was feeling. So much about Craig was exactly what she wanted, and yet she wasn't sure they could rectify their differences. She wondered if she should confront the issue of her tending wildlife with him and see what he had to say. Not this night, not on such a perfect Christmas.

"I think," she said, "that I could pack you up with the remainder of the goodies and you can go home to a nice night's sleep."

Craig nuzzled her neck with his face and then his lips. "I had another idea."

Nell smiled and teasingly pushed away from him. "I'm not surprised. I'll go wrap up that dessert."

Chapter Fifteen

Three days after Christmas, Craig telephoned Nell to ask her about dining out. After busy days at the clinic, she was not only receptive but also excited for the opportunity to see him again.

Over dinner they shared what they'd been doing for the past few days and decided it had been too much time between seeing one another. "I thought about you a hundred times," he said. "I go to sleep smiling thinking about our first-class Christmas together."

Nell agreed. "It was just the way I like it. So, have you been busy with work?"

Craig nodded. "I have. My company does analysis for companies worldwide – Japan, Great Britain, Belgium, India, and the United States of course. Sometimes the phone calls are at really early hours, once in a while late. Then I have follow-up work on the computer. I like what I'm doing. I trained for it in college, but this is the first job where I've actually used that education."

Nell ventured to say, "No more working with NAPS?"

Craig shook his head. "No, I liked the concept they

have, making sure wild animals are properly cared for, but this analysis work is up my alley, and no driving off to work. I get up, make coffee, take a shower, then I'm ready to begin the day. How about you? Anything new with your little fuzzballs?"

Nell smiled. "It's a mix of needs. Sometimes it's check-ups, sometimes it's an ailment. There's a woman who may need to forfeit her cat soon and if she does, I'm taking him. I've been holding off adopting a cat or dog to see what's happening. Her cat, Joe, is thirteen. I don't want to rattle his cage by bringing him to a house with another pet. Maybe later, once he's settled though. I'd actually like to have a few congenial creatures following me around."

Craig nodded. "That sounds like you and, actually, me too."

As they buttered warm rolls and waited for their meals to be served, Craig poured a second glass of wine for each of them. "I do need to talk to you about something," he began. "I need to take a few days to fly back to California. My company is based in L.A. and there's a corporate meeting I've been asked to attend. Typically I wouldn't need to go there, but since I'm relatively new to the job, they'd like me to sit in on the discussion."

Nell's heart threatened to jump through her chest. "Will you see your family?" she asked after a few moments.

"Unfortunately, no, they're a good three-hundred miles from the main office, and they're going to be away for at least one or two of those few days. I wanted you to know, and when I get back, we'll get together again for dinner or maybe a show in Bellowton. Unfortunately I won't be here to kiss you when the ball drops on New Year's Eve."

Nell was reluctant to say words that might stop in her throat. The thought of him going away, especially to the place that had been home, gave her a chill.

Their meals were placed before them and when the waitress had left their table, he looked at Nell. "Are you okay?"

Nell straightened her napkin across her lap and smiled. "Of course," she said cheerfully.

She understood that he was talking about just a few days, but it was so far away, and what if he reminisced and decided to stay there?

They ate their meals with casual conversation, Nell feeling like she had bricks in her stomach. Back at the cottage, Craig asked if she would like him to go inside with her or go along since it was after nine and they'd both had long work days.

"When are you leaving?" she asked.

"The day after tomorrow."

Nell swallowed and looked from her cottage to his wonderful face bathed in moonlight. "I have ginger cookies that were given to me as a gift. Would you like

169

some with coffee?"

Craig turned off the engine. "I'd love to join you," he said. "Is it too late for us to light a fire?"

Walking to the cottage door, Nell turned to him and explained that she was off for the next two days. "A fire would be perfect." She felt focused on the thought that this could be the last time she might see Craig for a very long time, if ever. What if he found himself in loved and familiar territory and rethought his move to the East Coast?

After shedding their coats and gloves across a chair, they walked to the kitchen. Nell handed him a tin box and told him to help himself while she made coffee. He took a cookie and savored the bite as he turned toward the parlor and stacked a small fire. When he returned, the coffee was nearly ready and he stood at the island to watch Nell place mugs and napkins before him.

"It won't be long," she said. "Just a minute or two to let it steep. I can smell the fire. It's so nice when there's a piece of cherry mixed in. I'm getting pretty good at knowing my woods."

Craig smiled. "Yes, you are. Ready for me to take the tray in where we can enjoy the warmth?"

Nell filled the two mugs then followed him with the napkins and tin of cookies.

"How long will the tree stay up?" he asked as they sat down. "I hate to see it go."

"It's just a few days before New Year's, and I'd

never let it go before then. My parents left their tree up until the day after New Year's Day. I'm leaving mine up longer, probably until Little Christmas, January sixth. But I won't want to give it up even then."

Craig took a sip of coffee and chose another ginger cookie. "It's your tree. You can leave it up all year if you want to. I'm afraid I'd have it up until Easter."

Nell smiled. "It's so pretty. I come in here every night and sit down to look at the lights and little white stars. There's something comforting about having a tree in the house, even though it's not one that was cut for the holidays. In fact, it's much more comforting that I didn't cause a tree to perish."

"You know what? We think a lot alike. I've gone by these lots where they sell Christmas trees and I see them stacked up, tied with rope. I always wonder how many birds were chased from their home. I'd never want anything other than an artificial tree – to me it's as real as the joy it delivers. And I love the hand-cut white stars. It's definitely a Nell McGann special."

Nell laughed. "I suppose it is."

They enjoyed more than an hour of coffee and pleasant conversation before the fire began to deliver a calming glow in the cinders. Craig sat with his head back on the sofa's cushions and Nell sat across from him. "You know," he said, "there's room for you over here next to me."

Nell didn't respond immediately. She allowed her

eyes to travel from his face to the hearth then back to him. "More coffee?"

"Are you trying to distract me?" he asked. "No on the coffee, thanks. I might just try for a decent night's sleep. I caught up on my work and don't have any meetings tomorrow, so I might even sleep in."

"And then you'll probably have to pack before going off. I hope you have an easy flight, no winter storms."

Craig sat up straight and finished his last few sips of coffee. He rubbed his eyes and looked at Nell. "I'll miss you."

Nell did not want the traitorous tears to fall and kept them at bay. "You'll be too busy," she said.

"I'll never be too busy not to miss you, Nell."

When he stood to slip his arms into his jacket and pull the gloves over his long fingers, Nell couldn't help but think of the fact that he'd be away for New Year's Eve. Not that the typical party night meant much to her. She'd been out for New Year's other times without any particular sense of enjoyment. It depended, she thought, on who you were with. After kissing her goodnight, he said he'd see her soon. Nell wondered how he'd spend the holiday, if there was the possibility of other plans he hadn't chosen to mention.

At the sound of his car engine, she closed and locked the door then leaned against its interior, her eyes to the darkening hearth. The cozy room now seemed depleted. What if this was it?

Nell walked to the light by her chair and turned it off then took their coffee mugs to the kitchen. She held his for a few seconds longer than her own, wanting to feel the connection she'd come to enjoy. He'd said he was going to miss her. She was going to miss *him.*

On New Year's Eve the phone rang and Nell ran to pick it up, thinking it might be Craig. It was Dr. Hill explaining an emergency and asking if she could meet him at the clinic. Nell changed into her uniform and drove as fast as she could the few miles into town. The emergency was a dog who had fallen over in his owner's living room seeming to have convulsions. After a thorough examination to a Collie-mix who seemed slightly bewildered but otherwise fine, Dr. Hill came to the conclusion that it had been a seizure, not uncommon in dogs and cats. A prescription for potassium-bromide was formed, and the dog went home with a relieved owner.

"While I have you here, Nell, I have this little issue and wondered if you could help. Yesterday a blue jay flew into one of our windows. I went out and brought him in from the cold. He was stunned and I knew he'd die out there from the temperature or a hawk. He's in a cardboard box at home in a closet. We made a nest with an old towel and left him bird seed. It's not the best situation though, especially with our cats being so curious, and I was hoping…"

Nell raised her eyebrows and looked at Dr. Hill. "I'm no expert with birds, but if you think it just needs peace and quiet for a day or two, I could take him home. If he makes it, we can release him in your yard."

Dr. Hill smiled. "I knew I could count on you. So glad you have a heart for these wild things. I examined him and found no broken wings or legs. I do think it's a concussion and that in a day or two he might show us he's ready to go. Could you stop by the house and pick him up?"

Nell smiled. "Yes, I will. I have clean cages waiting. Don't you wonder how many other birds and mammals face a tragic end when there's no one to help?"

Dr. Hill nodded. "I think about it a lot. Over the years I've done my best for wildlife, but other than our garage or basement, I haven't a good place to help them recover. I thought of building something just for that purpose years ago, but I didn't. I used to sneak them into the clinic, but that's risky."

Nell agreed. "I've considered becoming licensed. I've given it serious consideration, but I was told by a rehabber in California that once you're known for being one, you're open to unannounced inspections and sometimes an armful of creatures all at once. I still think about it though. Maybe some day. In the meantime, I'll stop at your house and pick up the bird – he'll have warmth and quiet."

Arriving back at her cottage before taking her own coat off, Nell gently moved the blue jay to a cage lined with Timothy hay. She added a small wool blanket, a heavy water dish with just a half inch of water in it, and seed. Leaving him in a darkened space was going to be the best chance for him to heal.

Quietly closing the door behind her, she walked to her front closet to hang her coat then went to her room to change out of her uniform and into warm slacks and a heavy sweater. She made tea and sat down with it, checking her phone for messages. Nothing. Nell sat back in her parlor chair and wondered what Craig was doing on this heavy date night in California. Then she realized that his being gone meant she didn't have to worry about him discovering her recovery room. That blue jay was one vocal little patient

She questioned why she had allowed Craig into her safe existence. There was no way it could work anyway, not with their different views on wildlife. She smiled hearing the complaints from the back room – it seemed he was getting better.

At close to midnight, with still no sound emitting from the phone, Nell took her telescope to the front window and searched the sky for the more brilliant stars. Clouds wanted to be the show and concealed much of what she hoped to see, but still, with her wonderful gift from Craig, she found at least part of the Little Dipper and other significant luminous, heavenly bodies. She looked for more than twenty minutes then hearing the clock strike midnight, and still no call, she placed the telescope down under the tree and prepared herself for a night's sleep. She felt disheartened recalling that last year at this time she'd had no expectations. This year was different. There should have been Craig.

On New Year's Day her parents called to wish her a happy New Year and to ask what she'd done for the evening before. Nell told of the clinic call for the dog and kept the conversation directed toward her work and winter in New England. She hadn't mentioned Craig to them at all. They, in turn, spoke of their evening at the home of a friend who had a small dinner party with eight friends. It sounded companionable and Nell knew they needed that.

When the afternoon sun began to fade, Nell decided that a short walk would be right and then maybe she'd start a nice fire with birch logs she'd been given by Dr. and Mrs. Hill. They'd lost a tree in their yard the year before and managed to save most of it for firewood.

Out in the cold she took a deep breath as she finished tucking a heavy scarf into her winter coat. With a snug knitted hat and warm gloves, she felt comfortable and was glad to be outside. She thought of her walk with Craig on Christmas Day and felt momentarily sad, but then she lectured herself on the fact that she needed to get accustomed to this, that she was a wildlife advocate, and there was nothing she could do about changing that. Craig would have to be second fiddle, or maybe nothing.

She stooped to pick up a few twigs and broken branches. They would dry nicely in the house and then would serve as perfect kindling for a future fire.

Inside the cottage again, she slipped her feet out of boots and hung her winter gear in the closet. Rubbing her hands, she walked to the kitchen, made coffee, then went back to the parlor and set up the hearth for a warm blaze. She felt fulfilled, a bit happy, yet a measure of loneliness.

With the flames starting to catch the old, dry kindling, she sat back in her chair and watched the fire. Her eyes to the flames, she couldn't help but think of Craig. He loved that hearth and cottage, as did she. They were, she admitted, a perfect pair, except for one thing, and one of them was chirping in her back room.

Chapter Sixteen

Over the next few days Nell was busy at the clinic as well as at home. She decided to cook and freeze two casseroles and, since she had frozen wild blueberries she would bake and freeze two blueberry pies. Nell had secured the berries, wrapped in layers of plastic, and now it seemed like a good time to use them. She envisioned Craig enjoying some, then scolded herself for thinking such thoughts. He hadn't called on New Year's Eve, not on New Year's Day, nothing. Obviously he was busy, but with what? The doubts she hadn't previously felt regarding past relationships were now distressing.

After three more days with no word from Craig and a long day at the clinic, Nell sat down feeling defeated. She'd tended to several little patients with success, yet coming home to a chirping bird didn't quite fill in the gaps left by Craig Vincent McGann. She had to find a way to replenish her life, she decided. She hadn't missed him before they'd met, so why should she now? He'd said that he'd miss her, but seemingly that wasn't true.

Nell finally decided that with her two days off, she

would paint. This time it would be a snow scene, one she had already imagined in her mind, and she would endeavor to put Craig as far away from her thoughts as California.

As she gathered her supplies, she chastised herself for being so disappointed. Craig hadn't told her that he'd call. Why had she expected him to? Because, she admitted to herself, she thought of him as her boyfriend. She had never given him any indication that she thought of him as such, but how could either of them think of the other as anything else? He'd practically proposed to her – twice. So it was her own fault, she determined, to have given him that measure of importance, to have pushed him away, to have allowed him a place in her heart that could be left vacant. She had not settled in rural Connecticut to find a man, after all. Maybe this was all for the best.

With tea at her side and her painting before her, Nell engrossed herself in thoughts of creating a scene that was familiar to the area. Every stroke to produce a wizened branch reaching toward a winter sky or falling to touch the pureness of ground snow, every Cardinal she depicted nestled on a pine, its scarlet plumes highlighted by the subdued hues of white and gray, encouraged her to think of a simple pastoral landscape. In her heart and mind, this was what she'd always wanted, always planned for, and then it happened.

She thought back to her childhood and early young

adult years in California. The life she had was ideal to many. Nell didn't think beyond her existence until she graduated from college with her vet tech degree. It was then, at twenty-two, that she began to think of owning a small farm, a remote place away from neighbors where she could consider having a pet pig, a goat, maybe a few sheep. And she thought about being capable of mending small forms of wildlife – squirrels, chipmunks, birds, raccoons. She felt for them, that they never knew a tender hand petting their soft fur, never felt entirely secure where something bigger and stronger could envelope them and threaten their lives. She was torn for her devotion to the lives of other creatures. Nell had grown to accept that she might never know love from a boyfriend, a husband. She daydreamed often about how that whole system could possibly work, unless she was fortunate enough to meet someone who felt the same. A child or two could be fun. She would teach them about compassion, how to take care in not stepping on ants, not catching butterflies. No one had taught that to Nell, but she'd felt it and figured it out for herself.

After more than two hours at the small easel Nell used at her kitchen island, she stopped, washed her brush, then made fresh tea.

The light was fading early on winter days and artificial light was simply not the same. Nell decided that the barn she'd sketched into the scene could be painted over the next day or two. She imagined it a traditional red, then wondered how it would look bathed in a burnt umber with golden highlights. She took a deep breath and decided that decision could wait. She was hungry.

With the painting project secured in a corner of her bedroom, Nell made a sandwich and enjoyed it by the fire along with a ginger cookie from Christmas. It was still delicious, although a little crunchier than it had been a dozen days or so earlier.

She thought about how much Craig had liked them and then she recalled that Craig liked everything sweet, although his form was lean, no evidence of extra desserts. She sat with her eyes on the blue and brilliant orange streaks of flame and thought of him, wondering what he was doing at that very moment. She had no idea if he was still in California or if he was back. It felt wrong not to know.

It began to prey on her mind how or why, if she meant anything at all to him, he could go for days and have no contact. Then she thought of illness or an accident. Every imaginable negative crossed into her thoughts and tortured her until she decided it was possibly something more hideous, like another woman. Not knowing was a form of torment. She willed herself to enjoy the fire with a good book. Craig would come back or he wouldn't. There was nothing she could do about his decisions. All she could control was to be sensible about their relationship and call it an interesting alliance.

At close to midnight, the phone rang and jarred Nell's thoughts as she struggled to wake up from her comfortable chair and a cold hearth. She heard Craig's voice apologizing for calling so late.

"I got to California and realized I'd forgotten my cell phone, so I didn't have your number with me. I tried calling the clinic and they wouldn't give me the number. It drove me crazy. Then the president and owner of the company I work for wanted the conference to go on after the New Year, so I was caught with no way to hear your voice. I'm so sorry, Nell. I thought I was going to be able to talk with you."

Nell took a deep breath and adjusted how she was sitting in her chair. "Where are you?" she asked.

"I'm in my apartment, but I'm dying to see you. Can I come over now or is it too late?"

Nell hesitated. "Did you have a nice New Year's Eve and day?"

"They were okay. Since we were stuck at the hotel, a few of us passed the time together. What have you been up to?"

She could tell by his tone that he was disappointed in her lack of response. But he'd been off *passing the time* with who knows what. She felt neglected and abandoned even though she knew she had no right to. "I worked part of the time, and I painted."

Her answer was brief and unrevealing. There was no way she was going to question him further. He was young and handsome, certainly she couldn't expect that he'd lock himself in a room when he'd had invitations to play.

"Is it too late for me to stop by?"

Nell looked at the clock, now after midnight. "It's pretty late."

The silence lasted for about half a minute but seemed like an hour. "Okay," he said, "but tomorrow, are you working?"

"No, I have the day off."

"Could we get together?"

Nell tried to think quickly. She wanted to see him more than anything, yet she was feeling both upset and foolish for having thought so much about him for the past several days. Now he was back having had days of party life in his home state.

"Nell, are you there?"

"Yes, I'm here."

"Are you okay? Can you spare me a couple of hours tomorrow?"

Nell wasn't sure how to react. To preserve her sanity, she'd convinced herself that things between them were over. She was falling, or had fallen, in love with this man and now she was afraid he'd decide that they weren't meant to be. "Sorry, yes, I'm fine. I think I'm still half asleep," she said. "Tomorrow then?"

"Yes, that's great. Will you have breakfast with me?"

Again Nell hesitated. "Sure. Where? I could meet you."

"No way," he said. "I'll pick you up and we'll head out to Shaughnessy's. We can talk on the way and then have a wonderful New England breakfast. I can't wait to see you."

"Okay, so about nine?"

"Nine works," he said. "I'll see you in the morning."

Nell sat with the phone in her hand and cried. He seemed like he was anxious to see her, yet he'd been gone and she'd imagined so many possibilities – none of them any good. Why was she working so hard to push him away when she wanted to hold him so close? She felt a pang of adrenalin at the thought of seeing him. He was important to her life. But would he accept her vocation to care for injured and needy wildlife?

She felt the urge to brace herself for a life alone, where she could seek peacefulness in her commitment to the welfare of animals. There were people in the world like her hero, Jane Goodall, who had made gorillas and other species her life's responsibility. There could be no form of altering that endeavor. It was deeply embedded no matter what other influence threatened to settle in.

Love, she knew, could be the cause of forfeiting

your values, relinquishing your beliefs, draining your soul. Nell would be discriminatingly precise, slow to allow affection to overcome her. And at the same time, she would be sound and quick to judge what she could and could not do.

Restless in bed that night, her eyes to the faded stars overcome by snow-filled clouds, she threatened to lose tears once again thinking about what the next day might bring. She closed her eyes and decided that she was not going to search the sky and she was not going to think more about Craig McGann.

With morning's light, Nell scrambled out of bed, took a quick shower, then made coffee. Her next move was to check on the bird, which seemed perky and hopeful for release. She called Dr. Hill and asked if he thought the blue jay might be ready? Then she realized that it was about twenty degrees, and suggested it might be too cold to put him out. Dr. Hill agreed and asked if she could keep him until the temperature rose to above freezing? Nell assured him that it wouldn't be a problem. Then she remembered Craig. The bird was not exactly voiceless. He made his well-known call every now and then, sometimes with a low but audible chirp. She was going to have to keep Craig away from the house.

When he arrived to pick her up for their breakfast jaunt, Nell met him at the door, buttoning her coat and pulling on gloves. He smiled at her and reached for her hand.

"You look beautiful," he said.

Nell's usual smile was missing and he noticed. They walked to his warm car where they strapped themselves in and pulled out onto the road.

Nell's quiet demeanor seemed troubling to Craig. He looked over at her as he drove and asked, "Are we okay?"

Nell looked out through hazed windows to the dark spindle branches against pale gray skies. She diverted her eyes when all she really wanted to do was look at his face.

"I guess so," she replied softly.

Craig glanced at her every few seconds while keeping his attention to the road. When they pulled into the restaurant parking lot, Craig kept the engine running and looked at her.

"Tell me," he said. "What's wrong? There's a tension between us taking up a lot of space. Is it because I was away longer than I'd expected to be? And because I couldn't call? Tell me, Nell, how do I fix whatever is broken?"

Nell's eyes glistened as she looked away. "I don't even know how to explain. It was longer than you'd said it would be, and then when New Year's came and you didn't call, I was just a little…I don't know what I was."

Craig reached over and clasped his hand over hers.

"I know. It was a bad situation having to be there longer, and then not having your number. I remembered parts of it, even dialed a number and thought I might reach you. It was an answering machine for someone else. All the way back on the plane I kept thinking that when I called the clinic I should have asked them to give you a message. When they wouldn't divulge your number, I was frustrated, Nell."

She looked away unsure of what to reply.

"I had the best Christmas of my life with you, and I would have loved bringing in the New Year with you. The timing was really bad. I'm sorry about that. I missed you."

"You had time to miss me?" she heard herself ask and wished she could slap herself.

Craig took a deep breath. "Yeah, I know, it must seem like I was off partying around and didn't give you a thought. But that's not true. I wasn't going to go to the gathering, but I caved in. It was pretty innocent, Nell. I was with my friend Dirk and his fiancé, a few other people from work. Dirk and I had interned together, so he was the only person I even knew. It would have been perfect if you'd been there."

Nell looked at him, tears brimming. He squeezed her hand and kept his eyes on her saddened expression. "Hey, two good things came out of this. First," he said. "I won't ever have to go there again for a conference.

They're expanding to Boston. If I need to attend a meeting, it will be just a couple of hours away. I'll be able to drive there and you could be at my side. Two, I've memorized your phone number, so I will always be able to call you. Now, let's go eat. I'm famished."

Nell found herself feeling better as they walked inside and were seated at a booth overlooking a half frozen brook. They ordered waffles and coffee then spoke of other subjects than Craig's trip to California.

Nell felt far more relaxed on their return toward her cottage. They pulled into her driveway and Craig shifted the car into park, leaving the engine running. "May I come in?"

Nell thought about the bird and decided it would be best if Craig stayed away until her feathered guest could be released. "We had a wonderful breakfast and visit, but don't you have work to do?"

"Yup, I do, but I'd still love more time with you if you're willing. A fire, hot coffee?" he begged.

Nell thought again of the bird. Maybe he'd be quiet, or if not quiet, maybe she could explain that she was caring for a bird for Dr. Hill. She didn't have to reveal that it was a blue jay. She could let him imagine that it was someone's parrot, a parakeet.

"I suppose a fire would be nice," she said with a trace of a smile. "Come on in."

They walked to the door together, shedding their coats and gloves inside. Craig stacked wood and kindling while Nell heated two mugs of coffee. When she took them into the parlor where Craig was poking at the fire to straighten hefty birch logs, he turned to look at her. She was, he felt, everything he could have dreamed of. Not just because she was blonde and pretty, not because she was living in a charming little cottage by an old cemetery, but because she was unique in her own expectations for life. She was not like any other female he'd ever known. No elaborate outfits, no manufactured hairstyle. She was evidently perfectly fine without fussing with her hair and her clothes, and her chosen place to live was far from what most young women he'd known before would choose. Nell – neighbor to a cemetery which she tended with respect and a caretaker to cherished pets – was the full package.

They sat down, she in her chair, he on the sofa. "This is my Heaven," he said.

Nell took a sip of her coffee and smiled. "I'm glad you like it. I love it here."

Just as she spoke those words, the blue jay squawked and Craig was startled. Nell couldn't help but laugh as her companion looked at her with a question on his lips.

"That's a bird Dr. Hill is tending to. He needed recovery time and I offered to take him for a few days to keep him away from the noise of the cats and dogs at the clinic."

Craig nodded. "He sounds a lot like a blue jay. How's he doing?"

Nell smiled. "You're right, it does sound a lot like a blue jay. He's doing well. Dr. Hill will be taking him back soon."

Craig asked nothing else concerning the bird, which gave Nell an opportunity to change the subject. "So, the business you had in California went well?"

"Very good. They're pleased with me, and I'm pleased with them. It's a people-oriented company. The owner has five kids, all under sixteen. He's a family type who turned in his sports car for a minivan."

Nell laughed. "Five kids in a sports car just wouldn't work, huh?"

After several silent minutes, Craig looked at Nell and set his coffee down on the table next to him. "I have reports I need to work on later today, but how does tomorrow evening look for dinner? You can choose the place. It won't matter to me as long as you're there."

Nell looked at him and was reminded how appealing he could be. "Instead of going out to a restaurant, how about if I make dinner for us here? I have frozen casseroles and frozen blueberry pies – I could thaw one of each and bake it."

"You don't have to ask twice," he said. "That sounds like a deal. Or, instead of the casserole, how about if I bring pizza? That way you don't have to cook. I can pick one up next door to my place."

"I'd love pizza. Cheese with pineapple on my half," she said.

"You've got it. I'll have it here at what, six?"

She agreed to the time and when he walked to the door as the skies were beginning to darken, Nell walked near to him. He turned, placed one hand at the small of her back and one to her left upper arm, pulling her into his arms. "Nell McGann, I can't wait to see you again."

Chapter Seventeen

Over the next several days Craig invited himself into Nell's life as she became a willing participant. She found herself aching to be with him and then asking the stars at night if things could really work between them.

She returned the blue jay to Dr. Hill's home on a sunny and near forty-degree day. The restless bird was released, and it flew to a tall pine in the doctor's backyard, seeming fine and relieved to be free. Both Dr. and Mrs. Hill were grateful to Nell for her good care as they watched with binoculars when there appeared to be a successful reunion. As he sat on a limb and looked around, another jay flew to him and they chirped to one another as though one was asking questions while the other was replying.

Nell found herself busy with the clinic and being at home where she kept everything neat, filling her hours with baking, cooking, and painting. Day after day she wondered how she'd been so lucky. The home she owned was perfect for her, and the man in her life was nearly so. He hadn't questioned the bird she'd had for over a week, thankfully never asked to see it, and no other little patients had come her way.

She watched every day for Daniel, Dennis, and Posey, her little squirrel babies. They were so big now that she could hardly tell them apart from the regular squirrels in her backyard trees. That was the good news when rearing little ones, that they successfully grew and skillfully mastered their intended environment. She knew that one day a small creature might not be well enough to release, and she would keep it safe for its lifetime if necessary. And this was where the issue with Craig could become a separating factor.

The snow seemed relentless in the month of February, which prompted Nell to clear areas at the base of her backyard maple where she could leave mountains of seed for the birds and squirrels.

Craig tapped at her door one afternoon carrying a large sack of sunflower seed from the local grain store. Nell smiled at his generosity as he placed a twenty-five pound bag just inside her parlor, then walked to his car for an equal amount of wild bird seed.

"Figured you could put this to good use," he said as he stepped inside, rubbing his cold hands.

"You're absolutely wonderful," she said. "I was running low and had intended to hit the grain depot by tomorrow. How about something hot to drink?"

"I would love that," he said while closing the door. "So, what have you been up to this fine wintery day?"

"If you start a fire," she said, "I'll tell you after I get us some coffee. Or would you prefer hot chocolate?"

"Oh, hot chocolate sounds great," he said as he stacked the hearth for a blaze.

When she returned with two mugs of cocoa, they sat down and he asked her again, "What was your day like?"

Nell placed her mug on the table next to her and sat back in her chair. "I actually went into the clinic for three hours. Dr. Hill needed help with two surgeries. Laura, who usually is there when I'm not, had to stay home. Her little boy has a fever. So, I helped with those two patients and then I came home to a long telephone call with my mom. After that I painted for about two hours. It was nice. How about you? What did you do?"

Craig sat back on the sofa and sipped the hot cocoa. "I started the day at six with a call to Sweden then I talked with my boss for about twenty minutes. He's giving me a promotion. That was a nice surprise. After that I did some analysis reports for about five hours before I needed a break. I ate half a leftover sub for lunch then went out to get the bird seed. The best part of my day is right now."

"You like your work. That's a true benefit."

"Yes, and so do you. I know your heart is with the animals. They're lucky to have you on their side."

Nell nodded. "So, when you leave here, where are

you off to? More work?"

Craig sat forward and gave her a wry smile. "Who said I'm leaving?"

Nell laughed. "Well, you're welcome to stay until the fire burns down."

Craig looked at her with questions in his expression. "What if I relight the fire? Then can I stay?"

Nell could feel her cheeks flushing as she gave him raised eyebrows. "Exactly how long were you thinking of staying, sir?"

Craig cocked his head to one side. "Forever sounds about right."

After several silent moments Nell asked, "It's nearly supper time. Could I interest you in soup and French bread? I tried a new recipe and it's not bad."

Craig smiled. "You don't know how to cook bad. I'd love to share supper with you. Anything I can do to help?"

"You could slice the bread and set the butter out. I'll heat the soup and set our places. After that, you're welcome to sit by the fire until it's time for you to go home."

Craig ran his hand through his hair and stood. "What if I don't want to go home?"

Nell turned to walk into the kitchen where she set a pot of soup on a burner to heat. "If you don't want to go home, I'll just have to put you out in the snow."

Craig followed then wrapped his arms around her

waist and kissed her neck. "Would you do that to me, blondie?"

"What do you think?" she asked with a smile as she turned to face him.

"Damn," he said. "I think you'd do it."

They laughed, hugged, kissed, then enjoyed Nell's delicious soup.

By eight o'clock Craig was falling asleep as the fire smoldered. Nell tossed him a blanket and told him to rest if he wished. "If you come over here with me," he said, "we could rest together."

With no further words, Nell walked to him and sat down, the warmth from their bodies being shared as he pulled her toward him, her head resting next to his neck. They stayed that way long enough that they both fell asleep and woke just after midnight.

"Wow, guess I was tired," Craig said. "Some of those early morning calls are causing me to lose my beauty sleep." Then he looked into Nell's sleepy eyes. "You, on the other hand, need no beauty sleep."

Nell shifted her position enough to stand and stretch. She reached for Craig's hand and tugged to pull him to his feet.

"You're making me go home, aren't you?" he said with his arms around her.

Nell butted her forehead to his then pulled back and looked into his beautiful eyes. "Yes, but not before you go warm up your car. I'll heat some more cocoa and then you'll be nice and warm."

Craig shrugged. "I'd be nice and warm here with you."

"Go warm your car," she said.

In the kitchen she heated one mug of cocoa for Craig and walked back into the parlor in time to see him coming through the door rubbing his gloved hands.

Accepting the warm drink from her he said, "Hey, we have a very special day coming up this month. We need some plans."

Nell looked at him quizzically. "What sort of plans, for what?"

Craig set the mug of cocoa down and reached out for her. "Nell, will you be my Valentine?"

She smiled. "Finish your drink. It'll warm your insides."

"Hey, you didn't answer me," he said.

"And if I decide to say yes, what do you have in mind?"

Craig finished his drink. "I was thinking we could go for dinner, a movie if you'd like, or whatever you might have in mind."

Nell buttoned the top of his jacket and tugged on his scarf. "I had nothing in mind, but I suppose we could dream something up. It's too cold to go star-gazing on the mountain, but after dinner, we could set up our telescope from my front or back windows and see what's out there in the winter sky."

Craig reached for her hands. "Starwatching would be every bit as much fun as a movie. We could enjoy a nice fire, too. Do you have a place you'd like to try for dinner? I should probably make reservations."

Nell loved the feeling of his large hands over hers. "What about keeping the evening here? Let me think...the 14th is a Friday, and I don't have work the next day. I could prepare us a meal of some sort. It might be kind of nice to stay in where it's warm."

"Are you sure? I mean, I'd love that, but it doesn't sound very generous of me to be taking advantage of your hospitality on Valentine's Day."

"You were invited," Nell said.

"Okay, so instead of you cooking, how about if I pick up dinner for us? What would you like?"

Nell squirmed and thought. "Hmm, I think you know that I love pineapple pizza. I'd like that and a salad, and I have wine. What do you think?"

"Wow," he said with a smile, "you're a cheap date. Are you sure that's what you want?"

Nell gave him a serious look. "I'm sure, unless you would prefer something else."

Craig shook his head side to side. "As long as I have you, everything else is perfect. It's a date."

Chapter Eighteen

That Friday of Valentine's Day aligned with Nell working until three in the afternoon. Expecting Craig at seven for dinner, she hurried home to make strawberry shortcake covered in mounds of whipped cream. She chilled a bottle of Riesling and another of Chianti. They would have choices to go with their meal.

At just before five she changed her clothes into something more festive than jeans and a sweater, an ankle-length dress in ruby colored flannel decorated with tiny white flowers. It had been a gift from her mother and one she had not yet worn. On her feet she wore red socks, no shoes. Then she remembered she had nothing as a gift for Craig. Hurriedly she brought her paints to the kitchen island and created a simple card – no words, but a rendition of little creatures holding a heart. Then she looked around for a possible gift. From her grandfather's collection of scarves, she selected one that looked new, dark blue with sketchy figures of trees in varying shades of blue and gray. She wrapped the scarf then left the package and card together on the sofa where Craig usually sat.

When Craig walked in near seven o'clock with a large bouquet of red roses, the pizza and salad, Nell accepted the blooms with a warm smile. "These are absolutely gorgeous. Come in and let me take the food while you hang your jacket in the closet."

"Oh," he said after delivering a kiss to her lips, "I've graduated to the closet rather than the back of a chair. This is looking hopeful."

Nell balanced the bag with the pizza and salad in her right hand while holding the bouquet in her left arm. Craig laughed when he saw her practically invisible due to the roses, then he reached for the food. "Here, let me take that while you find a vase for those."

He placed the pizza and salad on the set table and continued into the kitchen where he helped Nell locate a vessel that would be appropriate for the large bouquet.

She found an old piece of pottery that would work perfectly, filled it with tepid water, then placed her roses in, arranging them so that each one was visible. "These are so beautiful. Thank you, Craig."

He leaned forward to kiss her again and then they unwrapped the food, poured the wine, and enjoyed their meal.

"I'm stuffed," he said as they dabbed at their mouths with linen napkins. "But that was good."

"Too stuffed for some strawberry shortcake?" she

asked.

Craig's eyes lit up. "Give me a little while. I'm up to the challenge. How about if I start the fire going? If you poured us more wine, we could sit and simmer. And because you *are* my Valentine, maybe you'll sit next to me on the sofa."

"I'll get the wine while you make the hearth burst into magic."

Within moments, Nell walked into the parlor with two glasses of Chianti – they'd chosen Riesling with dinner. Craig moved from poking at the hearth to sitting on the sofa where he patted the seat next to him. Nell passed him his wine and then sat down so that their bodies were touching.

"I love that dress," he said. "You look like a Valentine in every way, and you're mine."

"Just a tad possessive, aren't you?" she asked after taking a sip of wine.

"You bet I am," he said, then he reached across her with his free hand and pulled her close, kissing her long and hard.

When he loosened his grip, Nell reached to her side for his card and gift. "This was a last minute sort of thought, and I'm sorry not to have shopped for something in preparation for this evening. But, I do hope you'll like it."

"Wait," Craig said as he stood and walked toward the closet where he'd left his jacket. He reached into the pocket and returned to sit with Nell. In her hand he placed an envelope and a small box. "There's this," he said about the card, "and there's this," he said about the box.

"Open yours first," she said.

"The lady goes first," he insisted.

Nell opened the card and found a romantic verse and beautiful design featuring flowers, a sparkling heart, and a trio of kittens. She looked at him and smiled. "You know me well." Her fingers tried not to disturb the pretty red foil wrapping on the box and the white ribbon. Once opened, she realized that this wasn't a nice pair of earrings or a sweet necklace, it was a brilliant and startlingly gorgeous diamond ring. Nell felt mesmerized, panicked, and speechless.

When she stared at the ring in silence, Craig wrapped his arm around her and leaned forward to look at her face. "This makes it real. We're genuine Valentines."

Tears slid from Nell's eyes. "It's the most beautiful thing I've ever seen."

"*You're* the most beautiful thing *I've* ever seen," he replied before pressing his lips to hers.

They sat quietly for a few minutes then Craig took the ring from the box and slid it onto her left ring finger. Nell looked down at her hand and shed a few more tears.

"So," he said softly, "you'll be my forever

202

Valentine?"

Nell looked at him, their faces just a few inches apart. "I think I always have been," she said softly.

Craig opened his card expressing the love for her work then placed the blue scarf around his neck. "I love this," he said after she explained it had been her grandfather's.

"I'll try harder next time to make sure I get to a store," she apologized.

"This is perfection," he said tugging at the scarf, "and you already know how much I love your art work. No store could out-do what you've given me, Nell. Plus we're going to have some of your shortcake, right?"

"Absolutely," she said. "Here or in the kitchen?"

"The fire is dwindling, so how about the kitchen? And maybe a hot drink? Coffee would be good."

Nell assembled dishes and spoons, cups for coffee, then lifted an ample bowl of shortcake to the island. Craig's eyes expressed his joy at seeing the mound of biscuits, strawberries, and whipped cream. "Holy smoke! There's enough for ten people there. This looks incredible."

Nell smiled as she cut into the dessert and put some in a dish then handed it to Craig. "You'll have to stop by again tomorrow and have more."

Craig nodded. "And I will."

Nell poured two coffees and sat down close to Craig

with her shortcake. "This has been an amazing night."

Craig swallowed some of his dessert and looked at her. "Have I told you how much I love you?"

Nell felt tears forming again and they laughed.

"I didn't mean to make you cry," he said. "I've been a little nervous about saying something stupid and making you angry with me. I bought the ring in California. I saw it and decided I was going to brave up and just give it to you. I am crazy about you, Nell. There's nothing about you that isn't perfect for me, for the life I envision. I'm just thankful that you think I'm a good fit for you, too."

Nell smoothed tears away and took a sip of coffee. "I love being with you."

Craig hesitated then said, "Look, I know I pounced on you with the ring, and I feel those reservations you have about me, but I love you more than anything, Nell, and I'm not going to pressure you. I want a life with you, right here in this fabulous cottage. We'll add more space and live here happily ever after. How does that sound?"

"I like what I hear," she said.

With dessert consumed they walked back into the parlor where the hearth was nearly dark with quiet embers. They sat together on the sofa. They held hands and kissed. Nell loved the elated feelings, yet they were mixed with concern. Craig was going to have to adjust to her taking care of wild little animals or this union wasn't going to happen.

"Are you tired?" he asked.

"Yes, but a good tired. I had a nice day and a fantastic evening. Thank you again for the roses. They're so beautiful."

"And because this evening was so incredibly right, I'm not going to ask you if I can stay. I'm sure I know what the answer would be, and I'm not going to push you into something you're not ready for. I'll behave and go back to my place, dreaming of the day when we're married and this will be my home, too."

Nell looked down at her ring. "It's funny: I came here thinking I'd be working for Dr. Hill, tending to the cemetery, and living in this house by myself. This ring changes so much."

"But you're happy?"

Nell nodded, "I'm happy."

Craig kissed her and then got up and walked toward the closet. He slipped his arms into his jacket, wrapped his new scarf around his neck, pulled on gloves, and found Nell next to him. He pulled her to him and whispered into her ear, "I'm so glad you're happy."

"Do you realize what we didn't do?" she asked.

"Oh, no!" Craig said with his hand to his head, "We never looked at the stars."

Nell laughed. "Wait, it's not too late. If you get my coat out of the closet, I'll get the telescope, and we can look while your car warms up a bit."

"Outside? It's freezing out there."

"I'll have my coat and you," she said. "Come on, we'll have a quick scan of the sky and then you can go along."

Craig helped her into her boots and coat before going out to a snow-covered ground and a brilliant star show. He started the car then they took turns looking at the sky, pointing out constellations and then bright Venus. After fifteen minutes they stopped when they heard an owl in the distance. Craig held the telescope, kissed her again, then suggested she go in where it was warm.

"I'll be by for more of that fabulous shortcake tomorrow."

Nell lingered holding his hand then let him go as she turned toward her door. Inside, she set the telescope down safely. Her heart was pounding. She looked down at her ring. This night was magical. Tomorrow she'd have to confront her greatest fear and risk losing everything.

Chapter Nineteen

At nine the next morning, Craig stepped up to Nell's door and knocked. He smiled as his bride-to-be opened the door, and he took her into his arms, dipped her back, and kissed her long and hard. When he set her upright again, he said, "I missed you."

Nell laughed and tried to catch her breath. "I guess so. And here I thought you were just back for more strawberry shortcake."

"If you insist," he smiled.

They closed the door to the blustery cold and walked hand in hand to the kitchen where Craig sat upon his usual stool. Nell poured him a cup of coffee and was filled with both joy and fear as she looked at this man she loved and played over and over in her mind how she'd tell him her truth.

"Thank you," Craig said then took a sip. "I swear, you make the best coffee. In fact, you make the best everything."

Nell laughed. "I'm not sure about the *everything* part. I think Grace has me beat on making breads."

"Hmmm…I won't put you to the test on that one, Mrs. McGann. But, if I could bother you for some strawberry shortcake to go with my coffee, I'd be very appreciative."

Nell gave him a wink and opened the refrigerator, removing the large bowl and placing it on the island before him.

"What? No spoon?" he asked, dipping his finger into the whipped cream.

Nell playfully slapped his hand then pulled a spoon from the drawer and slid it across to him. She sat down next to him with her coffee.

"How'd you sleep?" Craig asked after swallowing a bite of shortcake.

"Not bad," she teased. "How about you?"

"I'm not sure if I slept at all. I can't wait to spend the rest of our lives together." He reached over and squeezed Nell's hand. "Now, what are your plans for the rest of this beautiful day?"

"I haven't decided yet."

"How about a walk?"

Nell looked outside at the gently falling snow. "That sounds wonderful."

After each of them finished their coffee, Nell put the shortcake back into the refrigerator and they went to the front hall to dress warmly. Craig held the door open, and they went out into the winter wonderland.

Nell put her arm through his and they started down a trail that led off to the left of the cemetery. As they walked, Craig pointed to animal tracks and they laughed at some squirrels chasing each other among the branches, causing snow to fall. After about twenty minutes, Craig suggested they head back to the house and Nell agreed.

She tugged at his arm, leading him down another path. "It's a shortcut…sort of."

Craig raised his eyebrows. "Sort of?"

"Home is in this general direction."

"I see. Well, as long as I'm with you, I'm home."

After walking a few more minutes, Craig stopped suddenly. Nell looked at him, and he raised a finger to his lips. She joined him in quietly listening, and she heard a sound she couldn't identify.

Craig let go of Nell's arm and stepped carefully towards the noise. He moved further into the depth of forest, Nell close behind him. Then, without warning, Craig dove into the snow.

When he stood back up, Nell saw that he had a rabbit in his arms. She looked at him, stunned.

"Nell, something's wrong with this little guy. Looks like his leg is injured. Do you think Dr. Hill would be willing to take a look?" As he spoke, he carefully tucked the rabbit into his coat.

She was in total amazement, but this was her opportunity, and she knew she had to seize it. "I think he'll be willing. But don't you have someone from NAPS you should contact?"

Craig looked at her as they started to walk towards

the house. "Honestly, Nell, I think this little fellow just needs to be examined and then he'll likely thrive under your expert care."

Nell didn't quite know how to respond, she remained quiet.

"After Dr. Hill examines him, I think it's best for us to bring him back here. I can build a cage if we need to – I think he may need something a little bigger than what you already have. Unless your back room is only for squirrels and blue jays?" He laughed as Nell froze.

"You knew?"

"Of course," he responded. "Remember that day your door was open?"

Nell nodded.

"Well, I was panicked. And even though your car wasn't there, I went through every room in your house. Do you remember that I told you I called to you then closed the door? I did more than call your name, Nell. I was fearful you could be sick or injured or that someone else had broken in. I went into your house. I opened doors looking for you. I opened the backroom door you've always kept me from seeing. I saw three little squirrels, all in roomy cages, with fresh water and ample food and hay. I understand, Nell, that's an important part of your life. I'm with you."

Nell just stared at him, tears started down her cheek. "You've known all this time?"

"Yes."

"Did it ever occur to you that the reason I was pushing you away was because I was afraid how you'd feel about my not being in compliance with NAPS?"

Craig looked at her. "Nell, while I believe that NAPS does good work for the most part, they aren't the only ones who can help the animals. Now, if you don't mind, this rabbit just decided to urinate inside my jacket, and even though it's warm, it's cold, if you know what I mean."

"Damn you!" she said, laughing through tears. "I tried so hard to hide them, and I tried so hard not to love you." She took his arm and they headed toward the house with the perplexed creature, which was forced into a ready cage.

Craig smiled. "I'm with you one-hundred percent, Nell. Unless, of course, you start tending to bears. Then I might have to rethink our accommodations."

Nell looked from Craig's wonderful face to the frightened rabbit, then back at Craig. There were no words.

May the stars carry your sadness away,
may the flowers fill your heart with beauty,
may hope forever wipe away your tears,
and above all,
may silence make you strong.
Chief Dan George (4-28-20)

www.ingramcontent.com/pod-product-compliance
Lightning Source LLC
Chambersburg PA
CBHW020948180626
46814CB00003B/991